ELECTION 2008

ELECTION 2008

A Conversation in Heaven

THREE ACTS

Theresa Mohamed, Ed.D.

authorHOUSE®

AuthorHouse™
1663 Liberty Drive
Bloomington, IN 47403
www.authorhouse.com
Phone: 1-800-839-8640

First published by AuthorHouse   07/25/2011

ISBN: 978-1-4634-2924-9 (sc)
ISBN: 978-1-4634-2923-2 (ebk)

Library of Congress Control Number: 2011911515

Printed in the United States of America

Any people depicted in stock imagery provided by Thinkstock are models, and such images are being used for illustrative purposes only.
Certain stock imagery © Thinkstock.

This book is printed on acid-free paper.

Because of the dynamic nature of the Internet, any web addresses or links contained in this book may have changed since publication and may no longer be valid. The views expressed in this work are solely those of the author and do not necessarily reflect the views of the publisher, and the publisher hereby disclaims any responsibility for them.

Dedicated to the memory of my Siblings:

Georgette and Peter Bennerson

Acknowledgements

Thanks to my husband, Farouk Mohamed, for your continued support and encouragement.

Thanks to my children: Tasanna, Nalzon & Sherita Henry and Hemed & Rukiya Mohamed—you inspire me.

Thank you for your invaluable feedback on this work: David Feldman, Shirley Myrus, Sherita Henry and Hemed & Rukiya Mohamed

Thanks to my other siblings (the rest of the Bennerson clan) for a wonderful journey: Baraka, Marguerite, George, Helena, and Marcella; and my two cousins, Rosetta Cohen and Wilhelmina Dugue—family is strength!

I Died for Beauty

I died for beauty, but was scarce
Adjusted in the tomb,
When one who died for truth was lain
In an adjoining room.

He questioned softly why I failed?
"For beauty," I replied.
"And I for truth—the two are one;
We brethren are," he said.

And so, as kinsmen met a-night,
We talked between the rooms,
Until the moss had reached our lips,
And covered up our names.

—Emily Dickinson

Characters

John F. Kennedy
Robert F. Kennedy
Dr. Martin Luther King Jr.
Malcolm X
Unnamed Visitor (arrives in Act III)

The Setting

A room somewhere in Heaven on Tuesday, November 4, 2008 (Election Day)—it is the evening of the presidential election for the 44th president of the United States.

The scene is a large, modestly furnished living room/study with 60's furniture: a Ranch Oak Sofa with wooden arms sits in the center of the room, facing the audience. There is ample space behind and in front of the couch. Two matching Barrel Back arm chairs sit facing one another, angled at each end of the couch. A tall, narrow oak accent table is off to the right, near the back wall; On top of the table sits a vintage Magnavox AM/FM solid state radio. On the left wall, in the corner, is a 6-feet bookcase filled with an assortment of books. Adjacent to the left and right walls are book podiums, one on each side of the room.

Background

It is November 4, 2008, the first Black presidential candidate is on the ballot, Barack Hussein Obama, Democratic presidential candidate, and his running mate for vice president is Joseph Biden. The Republican candidate is John McCain, and his running mate for vice president is Sarah Palin, the first female Republican vice presidential candidate. It will be a historic election whichever party wins. Throughout the campaign, many people have echoed the sentiments as to whether or not America is ready for a Black president. In order for Obama to win, he must have the support of many White Americans.

It has been a particularly long presidential campaign due mainly to all of the dirty politics and smear campaigns. The Republicans have been in power for the past eight years, and the country is in the worst shape that it has been in for a long time: the country is involved in two wars (Afghanistan and Iraq), is in a recession, and unemployment is at an all time high, and so are gas prices. Americans are looking forward to change, whether it is with Barack Obama or John McCain.

Four remarkable men will come together to wait out the results of this historic election. In many ways they are the architects of what may unfold on this evening.

(Italicized text = actual statements made by individuals.)

ACT ONE

SCENE I

(The scene opens to a sparsely furnished living room. A tall, gangly, bespeckled black gentlemen dressed with a tie and jacket walks in from a door on the left. He pauses for a moment, looks around, and then walks over to the radio and turns it on. The announcer says that the presidential coverage will begin in a few hours. Satisfied, he promptly switches the radio off.)

MALCOLM
(He paces a bit, walks over to the front of the couch, then checks his watch, as he is suddenly thrown into deep thought. He begins to speak aloud to himself.)

Well, it's almost time for coverage to begin. I've waited so long for something like this. I can hardly believe this is happening. I could never have given White Americans this type of credit. For them to even allow a Black candidate to come this far truly represents some type of real change that I could never have fathomed, not in a million years. (Checks his watch again.) Come what may, history will be made tonight, whether the White man goes all the way or even if he stops short of electing a Black man, it will be the beginning of a new script that will have to be written.

(His thoughts and musings are interrupted by someone's entrance to the room.)

Dr. King, you made it.

DR. KING

Brother Malcolm, I told you that I would be here to join you on this momentous occasion.

>(DR. KING, dressed in a suit and tie, extends his hand as he walks toward MALCOLM.)

>MACOLM
>
>(MALCOLM goes to shake DR. KING'S hand but instead embraces him; it is a long embrace for both men.)

Yes, Dr. King, it is truly an extraordinary day.

DR. KING

That it is. I have waited a long time for the Dream to be realized.

MALCOLM

At the end of my life, I had began to hope that Whites and Blacks could join forces and work together to wipe out the evil that existed between the races, but this . . . , what's taking place today, is so astounding.

DR. KING

Of course it would be hard to imagine—the things we lived through were akin to a nightmare.

MALCOLM

Yes, you're right. The American Dream was a nightmare for Blacks. Something like this wasn't even on the radar.

>DR. KING
>
>(DR. KING is in an introspective moment and quietly shakes his head to what MALCOLM is saying.)

Brother Malcolm, yes, the 60's were truly a volatile period of unjust laws, segregation, lynchings, and race riots. It's hard to imagine we lived through all of that, especially after hundreds of years of slavery, and it's still not over.

MALCOLM
Just thinking about those incidents against the backdrop of what might happen tonight is what makes it inconceivable.

DR. KING
You are right. I remember the bus boycott with our courageous Ms. Parks leading the effort. Then there were those young Black and White college students who risked their livelihoods at the lunch counter sit-ins and on the freedom rides. How vivid those memories are, particularly at this moment. We thought that we had made progress only to be forced to take a few steps back each time. It was outrageous!

MALCOLM
Dr. King, are you thinking what I'm thinking?

KING
What is that?

MALCOLM
This election is so far-fetched to the both of us that it must be some more of that trickery from back then. We only think we are moving forward. A Black person shouldn't get his self all hyped up about there even being a chance of that man being elected tonight. What are we thinking? Why are we wasting our time here tonight, anyway?

DR. KING
No, Brother Malcolm, I don't believe there's any trickery going on here tonight. I am not really too surprised by what is taking place today in this election because I had a revelation.

MALCOLM

Let me get this straight. You had a revelation that a Black man was going to be a serious presidential candidate in America? Come on!

DR. KING

Not exactly, I didn't envision a Black man as president. But I saw the tremendous progress that would take place, and this is part of that progress. It was in Memphis, Tennessee, the day before I left my earthly life; I was facing an audience that day and giving a speech when it came to me.

> (DR. KING turns to face an imaginary audience and is transposed to an earlier time when he was giving the speech. He begins to mimic the words that he spoke at that time.)

Like anybody, I would like to live a long life. Longevity has its place. But I'm not concerned about that now. I just want to do God's will. And He's allowed me to go up to the mountain. And I've looked over. And I've seen the Promised Land. I may not get there with you. But I want you to know tonight, that we, as a people, will get to the Promised Land! (He returns to the present.) This progress had to happen. In my heart I knew that ignorance would lose its foothold.

> (DR. KING faces MALCOLM in an earnest moment.)

Brother Malcolm, I saw this day coming, but I knew it would take a lot more toil and struggle before it came. I finally believe that the train is pulling into the station of the Promised Land. That's exactly what's happening here tonight.

MALCOLM

Dr. King, there is still more toil and struggle to come.

(MALCOLM points his right index finger off into the air as he continues in a reflective moment.)

I would predict that this occasion is symbolic at best. It will be the beginning of a process that will take more time for full equality to take place.

DR. KING

Yes, that's a given, Brother Malcolm?

MALCOLM

If and when there is a Black president, it doesn't mean that racism and discrimination will cease being part of the Black man's plight. It is not going to be a magic bullet that cures all of the ills. That's what I mean.

DR. KING

Not overnight, it may not happen.

MALCOLM

You know how difficult it is to change someone's way of thinking when he's been thinking that way all of his life, and when he's part of the majority in power.

DR. KING

It is a very difficult task, changing minds and hearts that are set in their ways. I know that all too well. The Southern Christian Leadership Conference had its work cut out for it. It took sheer will and determination to carry out our work. There will always be the extreme groups, like the kkk.

MALCOLM

Exactly! Discrimination in the workplace or housing will not change overnight either because there's still a good part of this country that will be fighting against this type of change.

DR. KING

I am certainly in agreement with you, Brother Malcolm, but there has to be the first step.

MALCOLM

I was never patient with these baby steps. You know that.

DR. KING

Well, to tell the truth, I wasn't as patient as it may have seemed.

MALCOLM

You could have fooled me, Dr. King. It would take an enormous amount of patience to do the things that you did. You stood the test, all right, not retaliating after being attacked by vicious mobs, turning the other cheek, so that one could be punched too.

DR. KING

That is another story entirely. However, during the movement, I was merely being calm and focused, keeping my wits about me, so I could handle the business of a non-violent direct movement. I remember a statement that I made, and I was referring to patience and the tumultuous sixties. I said: *the Negro had never really been patient in the pure sense of the word. The posture of silent waiting was forced upon him psychologically because he was shackled physically.*

MALCOLM

Freedom is an elusive concept for the Black man, something he's always chasing, but never acquiring, like in your dream.

DR. KING

It was a dream that I chased. A dream, for me, that had shape and form.

MALCOLM

Dr. King, I applaud all of your efforts because your involvement in the movement was a tremendous sacrifice for you and your family. This day would not be possible without the work you put forth. Perhaps, I couldn't see the full breadth of your efforts at that time because I was in disagreement with your methods, but all was revealed in time. We wanted the same things, you and me.

DR. KING

Brother Malcolm, your sacrifice has also been great. And, America owes you a great deal for your honesty, integrity, vision, and courage. You placed the issue of race on the table for serious examination. Your contributions to the present day well-being of African Americans cannot even be counted. And, today, we stand here side-by-side to sow the fruits of our toil, and what a proud day this is. I am glad we decided to spend it together. (They embrace once again.)

MALCOLM

We stood on the backs of our ancestors, the slave who incited a resurrection on the slave ship or jumped overboard in protest, or the runaway slave, the Gabriel Prossers, Nat Turners, and Harriet Tubmans. In the grand scheme of things, the struggle was bigger than us, for we merely carried out God's will. We had only a small role to play in this tragedy.

DR. KING

Yes, indeed, Brother Malcolm, Amen.

MALCOLM

We have some time before the election coverage begins. Do you want to get comfortable over there? (Pointing to the couch.)

DR. KING
(DR. KING pauses for a moment as if bowed in prayer.)

Malcolm, I was thinking, since we have some time until the election coverage begins, let's get some fresh air before this spectacular event unfolds. It may be a long evening. A nice walk and a bit of reflection might be helpful.

MALCOLM
(Checks his watch and looks at the radio.) Certainly, I could use a brisk walk to ease this nervous tension.

> (DR. KING and MALCOLM exit through the door on the right.)

SCENE II

(After a few moments, two distinguished-looking blond-haired white gentlemen, impeccably dressed, step into the room through a door on the left. They have been chattering with a noticeable but slight Boston accent that hangs onto a few but not all of their words.)

JFK
(He stops in front of the radio and looks at it.)

Bobby, I thought Dr. King would be here by now. When I heard he was going to be here tonight awaiting the election results, I figured we would surprise him, walk in here, just to see the expression on his face. I was sure he would be shocked to see us. I got it from good authority that he would be here. I don't think he could have changed his plans. Do you think he changed his mind?

RFK
Jack, I am sure he will be here. He'll be surprised enough when he walks in here and sees us. (Laughs.) That's for sure. I am certain it will be a memorable evening. Let's sit down and wait for him. (They move toward the couch.)

JFK
I have so much respect for that man.

RFK
This night is important to you, huh, big brother?

JFK
Is it important to you?

RFK

Yes, I can't explain it.

JFK

It's because we were caught up in the midst of the Civil Rights Movement, and we have to see this thing through. It's something we carried in our hearts.

RFK

The sixties were an interesting period in history, aside from the music, dress and attitudes of the young people. Issues were being questioned like they never had before. Doing things just because they had always been done that way was definitely on its way out. Young people wanted answers that actually made sense.

JFK

But, what is going on today is the culmination of the struggle that took place in the sixties. It took all of that questioning to get where we are today. To have a presidential candidate who is Black is amazing. I am excited that even though I did not get to aid the movement as much as I would have liked, that this is happening now.

RFK

Yes, indeed!

JFK

Do you think it will happen? Do you think a Black man will be elected president of the United States this evening?

RFK

I think it can really happen. It is like what I said back in 1968. I remember the words exactly. (He reminisces.) *There's no question about it, in the next forty years a Negro can achieve the same position that my brother has . . . But we have tried to make progress and we are making progress. We are not going to accept the status quo.* How prophetic for me to make that statement forty years ago. I truly believed it when I said it.

JFK

You were right on the mark, weren't you? Bobby, even though I was not able to aid the movement as much as I would have liked, I have to admit that there is another reason that I am excited about this election.

RFK

What's that?

JFK

It was a moral responsibility, and I did not have the opportunity to see it through.

RFK

Yes, that's true. After you were gone, I tried to pick up where you left off. I was able to accomplish a few things, but not as much as I wanted. We were truly invested in this.

JFK

Yes, that's what I mean. You and I wanted this to happen, but our lives were cut short.

RFK

That doesn't mean our hearts weren't in it.

JFK

No, it doesn't. But that's not what I am trying to say.

RFK

What are you saying, Jack?

JFK

What I am trying to say is we are, today, still involved in this through our baby brother because it's a moral issue. Teddy is very invested in what's taking place tonight. And that means a lot to me. He knew our mind, where our hearts were, and he's taking a tremendous stand on this tonight. Don't you see? From the time Teddy took over my senate seat, he became part of it, following in his big brothers' footsteps.

RFK

Yes, I am excited about that, too. I am so proud of our little brother. This is his candidate tonight. Teddy has fully endorsed him and put all his confidence in this man. Teddy would not stand behind this man if he wasn't the real deal.

JFK

He continued where we left off. Don't you see? It took the teamwork of three brothers to get this straight. So, I am proud of our little brother. We have a lot to be proud of tonight.

RFK

Yes, with the culmination of all of our efforts, we certainly do.

JFK

I have to admit that it hasn't always been easy for Teddy, losing his three older brothers to violent and premature deaths. I think it put him into a tailspin for awhile, but in the end he devoted his life to public service and made us proud. Even with the Kennedy legacy, we weren't a perfect bunch, but we always did our best.

RFK

You began the process. I tried to pick up where you left off. I worked with LBJ to create the landmark Civil Rights Act of 1964. Teddy continued the work we started. It was important that we came here tonight to be with Dr. King.

JFK

(The BROTHERS put their arms around each other's shoulders, smile and give each other a pat on the shoulder.)

This is going to be a special evening, no matter how the race turns out. And we are here to see this through.

RFK

How it turns out is not our call. We are just observers now.

JFK

Yes, but we have always been partial to the Democratic Party and that doesn't have to change now.

RFK

Our little brother is finishing what we started or what we didn't have the foresight to contend with. This will be an exciting evening. We are very much invested in this thing, big brother.

JFK

You know my sweet Caroline has endorsed this candidate tonight as well.

RFK

So, I understand. She is her father's daughter, all right.

JFK

We are all so connected to this election tonight.

RFK

Yes, we are.

JFK

You know it is nice being here with you, Bobby.

RFK

Me, too. It reminds me of when we were kids, when we spent time in Hyannis Port, and the winters we spent in Palm Beach, with all the family together.

JFK

For me, I am reminded of the special time we spent together on that seven-week trip through Asia. You remember that, Bobby?

RFK

Do I? It was heaven being able to spend some time with my big brother like that, particularly with the experiences we had in those countries. I was glad I had my big brother there to share those transformative moments. I had a real worldview after that.

JFK

Yeah, since I was several years older, we weren't that close, but after that trip through Israel, India, Viet Nam, and Japan back in the 50's, we became best friends.

RFK

Yes, that time was really special for me. We bonded, and we have been a pair ever since.

JFK

Throughout my public life I came to rely and depend on you, especially while you were attorney general. If I wanted something done, I came to you. You were the one constant.

RFK

Jack, you can still depend on me. You know that.

JFK

I know that, Bobby. (Checks watch.) I sure hope Dr. King gets here soon, so we can all share the moment. The coverage is going to begin soon.

> (RFK goes over to the radio and turns it on. The announcer says some of the polls are about to close, and results should begin to trickle in soon. RFK switches off the radio. The BROTHERS sit on the couch, quietly in thought.)

SCENE III

(After a while the door on the left suddenly opens, and DR. KING and MALCOLM X walk in. They are in a jubilant mood, laughing and talking. Once eye contact is made between the four men, there is a moment of silence as the recognition process takes place.)

DR. KING

(Still startled.) Mr. President, is this really you? What are you doing here? I am a bit confused. Excuse me, and, Senator Robert Kennedy, too, it is, indeed, a pleasure. This is a coincidence, surely, for us to run into each other like this of all nights.

JFK

No, this is no twist of fate, Dr. King.

DR. KING

What do you mean?

JFK

I heard that you were going to be here tonight. Bobby and I figured we would surprise you. We didn't know that you made plans to share this evening with someone else. (Confusedly glances at MALCOLM.)

DR. KING

Well, I still would have to say it is a wonderful surprise. (Motioning to MALCOLM.) This is not just someone else that I am here with tonight.

JFK

(JFK looks at MALCOLM again curiously while continuing to talk.)

He does look rather familiar. Hello, how are you?

> (Extends his hand to MALCOLM while redirecting his attention to DR. KING)

But, Dr. King, you cannot deny that this is an auspicious occasion. Bobby and I wanted to be here to share it with you. We could think of no one that we wanted to share it with more.

> (With no reciprocation of a handshake from MALCOLM, he walks toward DR. KING with an extended hand.)

RFK

Yes, it is certainly an auspicious occasion. We knew you would be amazed to see us.

DR. KING

I am flabbergasted. This is incredible.

> (After shaking hands with the brothers, DR. KING gestures toward MALCOLM.)

I believe you are acquainted with Brother Malcolm here.

> (There is a brief tense moment between MALCOLM and the BROTHERS.)

JFK

Malcolm, I am sorry. I did not recognize you at first. No, I am not directly acquainted with Malcolm. How are you this evening?

> (JFK looks MALCOLM over a bit suspiciously as he extends his hand to him once more, a bit uncertain as to what he should expect. They reluctantly shake hands. RFK shakes MALCOLM'S hand as well.)

RFK

It's a pleasure to meet you, Malcolm. I've heard a lot of good things about you.

MALCOLM

Oh really!

JFK

I certainly heard many things about you during my lifetime, but never really got to know you.

MALCOLM

No doubt, Mr. President, I guess you can say we ran in different circles. No one would ever say that I could be speechless, but I almost am right now, seeing both of you here. You look a bit larger than life. (He grins.)

JFK

Maybe because we truly are now larger than life (Smiling.) This is an unexpected surprise to meet you here this evening, Malcolm. You were an up and coming young Minister with the Nation of Islam, as I recall, and, to be honest, we had very little in common in those days. Like you said, different circles, but it's good to see you.

MALCOLM

No, we didn't have anything in common, Mr. President. I take it that you had some things in common with Dr. King. Is that the reason you wanted to meet up here with him tonight?

JFK

In those days I understood where Dr. King's passion was coming from and why he took the course of action that he did. I believed in what he was doing and for what he stood.

MALCOLM

Did you understand my passion because both Dr. King and I wanted the same things for our people?

JFK

The passion but not the methods.

DR. KING

We did have our own approach. I will give you that, but those were desperate times that you couldn't personally know anything about.

JFK

I did know a great deal about the times, and I agreed with the non-violent approach used by Dr. King.

MALCOLM

And you thought I was violent?

RFK

You certainly had a fiery rhetoric.

JFK

You had very revolutionary ideas. That would not have been good for the country. It would have torn it apart.

> (The men are standing around the radio, MALCOLM and DR. KING on one side and RFK and JFK on the other.)

MALCOLM

(Walks toward JFK.) Well, let me ask you this, Mr. President, what did you think about the methods used by the Founding Fathers?

JFK

(Comes face-to-face with MALCOLM.) Like most people I have a deep admiration for them. They were an extremely intelligent and courageous group of men. The founding principles have stood the test of time.

MALCOLM

My methods were the same as the Founding Fathers. If you agreed with their methods, then you shouldn't have had any problem understanding where I was coming from.

JFK

Malcolm, I am not sure that I am following you with this discussion. I could not see how your approach was even feasible. The rhetoric frightened most people.

MALCOLM

(Points a finger in JFK's direction.) Did you agree with the revolution of 1776?

JFK

(In a stern voice.) I said that I had a deep admiration for the Founding Fathers and the actions they took.

MALCOLM

Very good, then, again, you should have understood my methods if you understood and respected their actions.

JFK

How were your actions and philosophy related to theirs?

MALCOLM

The Founding Fathers were seeking freedom and justice for the colonists. Were they not?

JFK

Absolutely! It was an undeniable quest for freedom, the ultimate sacrifice for them to put the colonists' well-being ahead of everything else. They were fighting for a God-given right, as Jefferson put it.

MALCOLM

Yes, exactly, because the colonists were being oppressed and treated like second class citizens. And as the Declaration of Independence says, It was their right, yet their duty *that whenever any Form of Government becomes destructive of these ends, it is the Right of the People to alter or to abolish it, and to institute new Government . . .* That was the philosophy that was finally agreed upon by the Founding Fathers, was it not?

JFK

Yes, it was, and I think the Declaration has stood the test of time, as well.

MALCOLM

Yes, but there were ideological consequences to what Jefferson wrote once Black people became citizens. Granted they were not included for in the Declaration when it was initially drafted. However, from where I stood, there was an enormous breech in the system for Blacks once they became citizens because they were being denied the same basic rights as White citizens of the United States. In the sixties Legislation was being passed for Black citizens of this country who were born here. Blacks had the right of birth but were still not qualified. It was a racist denial of a Black man's citizenship, I say. It indirectly said to the Black man that his citizenship would never be acknowledged.

DR. KING

(Steps between MALCOLM AND JFK's heated discussion.) I agree with that statement, Malcolm. Laws were being applied arbitrarily to keep Blacks enslaved. The Black man was supposed to be grateful for legislation that was passed to give him rights. *The basic rights he ought to have inherited automatically centuries ago, by virtue of his membership in the human family and his American birthright.* Do you deny that, Mr. President?

JFK

I agree on that point, gentlemen. But tell me, Malcolm, how do you equate your actions with those of the Founding Fathers? I would like to get to the illustration of that point.

MALCOLM

Okay, I'm getting there. (Steps in front of King to face JFK directly.) You see, many people didn't agree with my methods because they made the mistake of thinking that I was a Civil Rights leader, like Dr. King. Quite the contrary, I was a revolutionary concerned with human rights, just like the Fathers. If revolution was good enough for them, then it should be good for the millions of Black people suffering in America. Wouldn't you say?

RFK

(Steps between MALCOLM and JFK.) You know, Malcolm, I became better acquainted with your stance and rhetoric than my brother because Jack was taken away too early. I followed your activities and even read some things about you after your passing. It was then when I got to understand you a bit more, although I, too, had a greater preference for Dr. King's methods. They seemed more feasible at the time. But I did admire the fact that you were a self-made man. You had a very rough beginning and transformed your life. And I can see some of the parallels that you are drawing here between yourself and the Founding Fathers.

MALCOLM

(Laughs.) Okay! Why don't you tell it then?

RFK

Let's take one of the Father's, like Benjamin Franklin, for example, you had a lot in common with him. I am very familiar with his autobiography and life, so I will start there.

MALCOLM

Oh, really! Wow, that is a Founding Father that I would not have picked. Just on appearance alone, there's a radical difference. (They all laugh.)

RFK

Yes, you both started from meager beginnings and acquired immense popularity.

21

MALCOLM

Are you saying we fall into the category of a Horatio Alger story?

RFK

Pretty much! It is the story of young men rising from humble beginnings.

MALCOLM

Okay, so we both started from impoverished backgrounds and make good on it, what's next?

RFK

Yes, but it goes further than that. In many ways, you have a lot more similarities: it's more than just the common man who aspires to greatness and who exemplifies genius.

MALCOLM

Oh, I am definitely going to take that genius part as a compliment. (Smiling.)

RFK

You and Ben Franklin also wrote very significant autobiographies that benefited many young people and generations to come. Franklin wrote his autobiography as a moral source book so that those young people who would come after him, would have a guide and a way to uplift their lives. While your autobiography was written for the benefit of young Black people, mostly, but read by so many groups. You gave them a head start with the knowledge that filled your autobiography. You already made the mistakes, so they didn't have to. It gave them a good understanding of the racist society in which they lived. That is why the book remains so popular.

MALCOLM

Okay, I get it. I am the one who initially made this connection to the Founding Fathers with the fact that I had a revolutionary agenda, and now you are taking it quite a bit further with your analogy between old Ben Franklin and me.

RFK

Why not? You can see the similarities. Shall I continue?

JFK

Please do, Bobby. I am beginning to get a better feel for Malcolm and his ideas.

DR. KING
(DR. KING walks over to check the radio to see if the election coverage has begun. It has not.)

Do continue, Senator. We have some time yet to get better acquainted, and this may be a good way to warm up to one another. I'm looking forward to an enjoyable evening, so we might as well get all of the pleasantries out of the way.

MALCOLM

Please, Senator, indulge me.

RFK
Okay, then!

(RFK motions for the men to have a seat, RFK and MALCOLM sit on opposite ends of the couch and JFK and DR. KING in the chairs.)

Well, like I said, Malcolm, I was around for a few more years after you departed, and many of the distortions surrounding your life began to come to light.

DR. KING

That they did. I even began to appreciate some of your methods.

MALCOLM

What distortions, specifically?

RFK

Okay, let me continue with my analogy? I believe that I was building on your similarities to the Founding Fathers, particularly, Ben Franklin. So, besides the meager beginnings and significant autobiographies, which highlight that one can start at the bottom and rise to the top, the books reveal the errors and misdeeds of your early lives so poignantly. Of course there is a clear distinction between the two of you: Franklin is viewed as a victor and Malcolm as a victim. Yet, there is a common and crucial thread that binds you two and that is the undeniable quest for freedom and the fight against injustice in order to enjoy the basic civil liberties that make man a man and not a lower animal. How am I doing?

MALCOLM

I am impressed. You do have some understanding of my motives. Black people were being treated like animals.

DR. KING

Please continue, Senator.

JFK

Build a stronger case, Bobby, for why Malcolm's efforts should be ranked among those of the Founding Fathers.

RFK

Alright then, let me see. I notice that Franklin and Malcolm had a strong belief in education and both were self-taught. Franklin skipped meals to buy books and skipped sleep to practice prose. He clawed for knowledge, it has been said. He eventually set up a library and university.

MALCOLM

Those are things I never had the power or means to do, so we may need to stop here.

RFK

Well, no, because you began your intellectual development in prison, copying words from the dictionary. You became an avid reader and felt education was essential for young people. In 1964, you went to Paris and spoke at the Salle de lat Mutualite. From there you went to the UK and participated in a debate at Oxford. It was big news in the states and was televised.

MALCOLM

Yes, I did go the Oxford Union. I remember the debate that I participated in at that time. The topic of the debate was "Extremism in the Defense of Liberty is No Vice; Moderation in the Pursuit of Justice is No Virtue." I argued the affirmative.

RFK

You see the similarities. You did not establish a university, but you helped to inspire a movement, and under your leadership, the Nation of Islam grew from hundreds to hundreds of thousands.

JFK

Franklin was a slaveholder; how do you reconcile such a difference?

DR. KING

That is true.

RFK

There is no denying that Franklin was a slaveholder, and, at one time, Malcolm hated all White people. Both men were dogmatic in their thinking when it came to the opposite race.

MALCOLM

My early interactions shaped those views, the kkk forcing my family out of Omaha, our house being set on fire, my father's savage murder, the White insurance agent cheating my mother out of the insurance money, and the White social worker who separated the family. It's all in the autobiography. I was treated as little more than a pet in my White adoptive family's home. In school I was the only Black, and my peers felt I was beneath them. Then, there was my eighth grade teacher who said I needed to be realistic about being a "nigger." I made the mistake of telling him that I wanted to be a lawyer. I dropped out of school right after that.

RFK
It is fair to say that Franklin was somewhat repulsed by the black race, so you have that in common, hatred of each other's race. However, Franklin overcame much of that the same way that you did. He set up a school for slaves and actually marveled at their intelligence and acuity. He eventually signed the Memorial to Congress for the abolition of slavery and wrote articles in the press against the practice of slavery.

MALCOLM
My thinking about Whites did evolve. I remember saying that they could help us but could not join us. It was after the trip to Mecca and travels through Europe and Africa that I changed my thinking about the White population. I no longer generalized them as being all bad. I was eager to work with them, I said, *as long* as *their aims and objectives are in the direction of destroying the vulturous system that has been sucking the blood out of black people in this country.*

JFK
Well done, Bobby. I believe you have made your case. You have shown the progression of two great minds over time. Both men progressed politically, morally, and intellectually.

DR. KING
Congratulations, Brother Malcolm, you are ranked among the other great men of our country who stood for freedom and equality by any means necessary.

RFK
Yes, who knows what you may have gone on to do if you had lived to eighty-four years of age like Franklin? You left at the mere age of . . . .

MALCOLM
Thirty-nine. I was thirty-nine.

RFK
Yes, thirty-nine, who knows to which political office you may have aspired.

MALCOLM
You have made quite an impressive case, Senator. But I don't think anyone was going to elect me into political office.

RFK
Shall I compare you to Jefferson now. He was quite a bit of a statesman, you know.

MALCOLM
No, why don't we stop while we're ahead? I had many issues with Jefferson's personal lifestyle anyway. He might have more similarities with Elijah Muhammad in that area.

JFK
Aside from his personal lifestyle, what do you have to say about the man?

MALCOLM
(MALCOLM looks at his watch, rises, and goes over to the radio. A few exit polls are being looked at but no final numbers. He redirects his attention to JFK's question and sits back down.)

We know that Jefferson believed that democracy and the American dream were not meant for Black people, in light of what he saw as their pronounced inferiority, so that's enough for me to know about the man.

DR. KING

I am certain he wrestled with his conscience. He knew slavery was wrong and that the real basis was economic.

MALCOLM

He did not stand on principle, did he? The only thing Jefferson did was to try and blame slavery on the British for introducing it into the colonies. Slavery was essential to the southern way of life and a large part of its economy, and he could not put the mighty dollar aside to do what was moral.

DR. KING

Please, let me add my conclusion to the similarities between Malcolm and the Founding Fathers. Like Jefferson and the others, they knew that freedom came at a price. It was worth fighting and dying for. You, too, Malcolm, felt that you had to be ready to die for freedom. Yes, you were a revolutionary in the same spirit as these men. No one can argue with that.

MALCOLM

Ben Franklin got to be on the hundred dollar bill. I have not been so honored.

RFK

Well, I understand that your likeness has been issued on a postage stamp. There you go. All of the distortions had to be removed for that to happen.

JFK

Speaking of similarities, I understand that I have a lot in common with Candidate Obama.

MALCOLM

(Looking disgusted.) How do you have similarities with Obama? What do you have in common with a Black man?

DR. KING
Malcolm, I know you have transcended the race issue, like you said, so let's allow the president to explain.

JFK
Malcolm, why can't I have a few things in common with a Black man, if you can have so much in common with a group of old dead White men like Franklin and Jefferson?

MALCOLM
Did you really just say that, dead White men?

JFK
Okay, that was not a good choice of words.

MALCOLM
Let's back up here. I didn't mean to get defensive about you comparing yourself to Obama, Mr. President. But here we have the first Black presidential candidate who has gotten this far, and a White man wants to claim him, if that don't beat all. There's a surplus of White presidents, dead or alive, and Founding Fathers, for that matter, so it doesn't make a difference if I take a few of them, but you can't have Obama. White folks can't claim him in this one.

JFK
Well, that's what I am hearing. People of all colors are excited about his candidacy, and many are saying that he reminds them of me. I even hear that my sweet Caroline has been saying that people have come up to her and said Obama reminds them of a time in this country when John Fitzgerald Kennedy was running for president, and people were filled with hope and a promise for real change for the future. They said they haven't felt this way in a long time.

RFK

There has been some of that talk out there. People are energized because Obama reminds them of JFK, and they are ready for change.

MALCOLM

Actually, I was thinking that he reminded people of me.

DR. KING

How so?

MALCOLM

Don't tell me that you all haven't noticed it. Those oratorical skills that he has are similar to mine, the way he projects his voice, standing up there tall and lanky, like me. If you put a beard on him and a pair of glasses, that's me.

> (Everyone laughs, including MALCOLM. The radio is playing low in the background. Dr. KING goes over to turn it up. The first results are coming in. The announcer says that many of the northeastern states, like Maine and Vermont, New York, and Pennsylvania have gone to Obama as expected. He has also won Ohio and Indiana.)

JFK

Whether or not I am similar to Obama, I didn't win most of those states, only New York and Pennsylvania. This is going to be an interesting election. I wonder if we might all be able to settle down and share this evening together.

> (MALCOLM and JFK look suspiciously at one another.)

DR. KING

I don't think there is any reason we can't all share this evening together. (Looking at MALCOLM for agreement.)

MALCOLM

A few things still concern me and perhaps we can address them later, I guess. But, for now, I am willing to give it a try since the results are beginning to come in.

ACT TWO

SCENE I

(The scene opens as the men are seated ruminating over the election results. The KENNEDY brothers are sitting across from each other in the two arm chairs while DR. KING and MALCOLM are seated on opposite ends of the couch. It is then announced that Massachusetts, Connecticut, and New Jersey have just gone to Obama and South Carolina and Georgia to McCain. The mood becomes even more pensive as the men all silently process the latest results that have come in over the radio.)

KING

It is turning out to be quite an election.

RFK

I would say so.

JFK

I am taken aback by these results.

MALCOLM

I don't quite know how I am feeling right now and that bothers me.

DR. KING

What bothers you?

MALCOLM

Us, we are sitting here like this is normal and all, when really, we are the unlikeliest group to come together to wait for election results, particularly where a Black man is a candidate. It's just too weird.

RFK

Why does it have to be weird?

MALCOLM

We held such divergent views and were seldom in agreement on much. Now, we are just going to sit here like we are best friends without any explanation about the past.

> (MALCOLM directs his comments to JFK by letting his eyes finally rest on him.)

JFK

(Picking up on the tension.) You are absolutely right! If we were back in the 60's, we would be the unlikeliest group to be sitting around together. Sure, Bobby and I might be keeping company while we listened to the election results, but I don't even image you (Motions to MALCOLM.) and Dr. King waiting for the election results together, major philosophical differences there as well.

RFK

We are sitting here together because we have the benefit of being able to see the bigger picture now. We are in that special place, aren't we? (Nods his head for agreement from the others.)

DR. KING

This is a special place, Senator.

JFK

We ought to be glad we ended up here.

MALCOLM

Yeah, I am glad I made it here, by the skin of my teeth, I'm sure.

RFK

Besides, in the 60's we were all placed in somewhat narrow confines, as far as our thinking was concerned; meaning we might not have taken it upon ourselves to seek each other out for companionship, but, I think, we had fabulous thoughts about the changes that needed to be made in our society in regards to race relations.

MALCOLM

(Stands up and walks in the direction of JFK.) Yes, we do have the benefit of seeing the bigger picture, but we still have some unresolved lingering issues to address. Back then in the 60's, Mr. President, I have to admit that I didn't have a high opinion of you.

JFK

I think I figured that out by now.

MALCOLM

At one point I saw the whole country as one great big plantation and the president of the country as the plantation boss, yeah, you. (Looks at JFK.) Black people were suffering, and the president basically stood by and didn't do anything, maybe applied a band-aid on a major life-threatening wound. That's how I truly felt. Now, this is a wonderful occasion and all, and we are all excited because history is being made this evening just by the fact that a Black man as a presidential candidate has come this far. And it will be an even more tremendous occasion if he wins, no doubt. However, I am not going to ignore the elephant in the room all night because I just can't stop wondering why you didn't do more sooner, and why you felt it was important to be here with Dr. King this evening. Basically, you have some explaining to do.

DR. KING
(He rises and goes over to face MALCOLM who is still standing over a seated JFK.)

34

Malcolm, in all fairness, he was sympathetic to the cause, and all has been said and done. The past is the past, and we cannot change it. We can't even shape the future any more than we already have or that our legacy will permit.

MALCOLM

Dr. King, what do you call being sympathetic? Are you back to turning the other cheek? Black people were catching hell. Excuse my terminology.

DR. KING

No, my cheeks are worn out, but let us keep the discussion on an intellectual level.

MALCOLM

Dr. King, we were getting along just fine until these two showed up.

JFK

(He rises to face MALCOLM, interrupting his conversation with DR. KING.)

Malcolm, I wanted to do more. I just ran out of time. I hardly had a chance to get started.

MALCOLM

You ran out of time. Is that your excuse? Black people put all of their faith in you. Do you know what that means? They were waiting for you to deliver on your promises.

JFK

Of course, I know what that means. I was a politician, and politicians make promises. I made a lot of promises. Those promises were really part of my vision for the country. When I made them, I had every intention of carrying them out. However, I didn't make the world the way it was. I was just like everyone else, born into it.

MALCOLM

Is that another excuse, you didn't make the world? (Throws up his hands in despair and turns away.)

JFK

No, I didn't. It had flaws, and I merely wanted to make a difference. That's why I ran for president, but no one is perfect. Of course, I thought that it was horrendous the way Black people were being treated. I wouldn't have been able to live with myself if I didn't deliver on those promises, and I had every intention.

MALCOLM

Then what happened? I say you were moving too slowly, not that you ran out of time. There was no release for the masses of Black folks. They were suffering, economically, politically, and socially. Black people were tired of being the victims of hypocrisy in America. They were promised one thing during a campaign; they fell for the okey-doke, but it always turned out to be just a bunch of empty old promises, time after time. I think that's what made me so angry. I was given the moniker of the angriest man in America. You know, I had every right to be mad.

RFK
(He stands and joins the men and reaches out to touch MALCOLM'S shoulder.)

Malcolm, I do understand why you would be so angry. There were so many injustices being done to Black people, but I would have to say that it was a lot more complicated than you make it out to be. You make it seem that the president had some magic wand, and he could just do away with all of the structural inequities.

MALCOLM

Of course, you would say that it was a lot more complicated since your brother didn't fulfill his election promises.

RFK

Listen, I was the attorney general during my brother's administration, and I can attest to the difficulties that existed during those times, and I believe you are familiar with some of them.

DR. KING

It is true, Senator. Race in America was and remains a very complex issue; nevertheless, I would have to agree with Brother Malcolm that one of the major campaign promises, and I have every respect for you, Mr. President, was for you to use the stroke of the pen to wipe out housing discrimination immediately. We waited and waited and waited. When it finally did happen, years later, it was like being tossed a bone. Blacks were still no better off. Blacks still had a hard time obtaining financing and having laws implemented on their behalf. Everything moved in a snail-like pace, and when a man is drowning, he cannot wait for the right moment to be thrown a life preserver. Negros put their faith in the president by giving him a majority of their votes. I wouldn't say that the president betrayed his promise. It just took him awhile to rise to the level of his moral commitment.

JFK

I am not here today trying to make excuses, and I am happy to get this all out in the open. I think it is an important thing to do but when I came into office, I had a lot on my plate. I guess you could say comparable to the issues that will be facing the new president that will be elected today: the Vietnam War, the economy, and unemployment—similar issues. Then there was Cuba and the Soviet Missile Crisis. Everything and everybody needed my attention. Then, if you recall, it was a very close election. I won by a very narrow margin. I still needed to garner more support for some of my initiatives.

RFK

It was a close race, big brother. It was 49.7% to 49.6%, one of the narrowest elections ever; the country was split. I hope tonight's election won't be that close.

JFK

It could have gone into a recount; it was so narrow. My opponent would not hear of it since he felt the stability of the country would be at stake in such an endeavor. So, I had my supporters but also an equal amount of detractors.

MALCOLM

What does that have to do with your election promise? You are the president, and you can effect change, and I am not talking about waving a magic wand.

JFK

Well, for one, it's because I faced a lot of obstacles in just getting elected is what I am saying. A lot of it had to do with the fact that I was the first Irish president and the first Catholic one at that. The Irish didn't have it so good from the beginning in this country, so I understand a bit about discrimination. Why, my great-grandfather came to America during the potato famine with nothing. And being Catholic got to be quite a contentious issue during my campaign.

> (He continues with a faraway look on his face.)

I remember having to finally stand up and say, *I am not the Catholic candidate for president. I am the Democratic Party's candidate for president who also happens to be a Catholic. I do not speak for my church on public matters—and the church does not speak for me.* (Returns to present.) It took a while to convince enough people that being Catholic wasn't a negative attribute.

MALCOLM

So, you got through that okay. You convinced the country that being Irish and Catholic were a safe bet. They accepted that. You were narrowly elected. Then what?

JFK

Yes, evidently that got worked out for the most part. Like I said before, there were so many issues that needed my immediate attention once I got elected.

MALCOLM

What was so important that the Black man had to be added to the bottom of the pile?

DR. KING

Yes, let's have a final airing of the facts.

JFK

Where do I begin? Shortly after being in office, I went head first into a battle with the CIA. The CIA and the Pentagon were ruling powers back then, not like today. They don't have nearly as much control. Taking them on was like opening up the proverbial forbidden box because I had to practically declare war on the CIA. I felt they were working against me, giving me false information in order to manipulate me. And if that wasn't explosive enough, I sought to restructure the Federal Reserve in order to save the country a lot of money. The bankers were another powerful group in the country that did not take kindly to such reform, but I believed the economy was being manipulated. Then, I wanted to end the Viet Nam War, and some groups were against that because there were billions in armament sales tied to the war. I seemed to be making a lot of enemies in a short amount of time in my effort to bring about reform to the country. I also had to continually gain and retain the people's trust in all of these endeavors. It was quite a balancing act, to say the least.

MALCOLM

So, Mr. President, would you say that you were a bit naïve about the real nature of America?

JFK

Were you naïve?

MALCOLM

Touché! I do know quite a bit about the CIA and the FBI from that time. They were, indeed, their own branch of government, not to be underestimated.

JFK

Again, the Civil Rights movement was very much a concern of mine. Even though it didn't look like much was being done publicly, doesn't mean that the groundwork for some change was not being laid out.

DR. KING

It seemed as though it was the last thing on your list, Mr. President. A drowning man could try to float for awhile, tread the water, bide a bit of time if he knows he is certain to be rescued, but after a while hope begins to erode, and without hope, you know, there's nothing left.

JFK

As you gentlemen know, Civil Rights was a very unpopular issue. The country was still very much divided over what was the right thing to do when it concerned Black people. State rights', particularly in the South, was still a very touchy subject. The South did not want federal interference in their affairs. They made that very clear. Also, there were several issues I had to try and resolve first. I did not want to alienate the people whose support I needed on the pressing agenda of keeping this country together by bringing in the subject matter of race that was certain to divide the country. That wouldn't be the best strategy. In the words of President Lincoln, "A house divided against itself cannot stand."

DR. KING

Déjà vu—just like during Reconstruction—the Negro was still a problem 100 years later.

MALCOLM

Granted you were in a very difficult position at the time but when a group of people are suffering, they don't want to hear about the need to strategize to give them rights that ought to be theirs to begin with. The Colonists didn't want to hear about any difficulties that King George and the Parliament were going through before they could be treated like citizens. The colonists wanted freedom and equality right then and there. You understand?

JFK

Yes, I do. In those terms it is very clear. But you cannot judge a man when he is cut down in his prime before he's able to complete the tasks set before him. I did not simply choose not to fulfill my obligations.

MALCOLM

You were a very popular president, but not popular enough to escape the climate of America. I got a lot of flak for a comment I made after your assassination. I was asked a question by a reporter. I told him that the president's death was a case of the *chickens coming home to roost.* Of course, my comments were taken out of context. For me, it was clear that there was a climate of hate in the country. I was not happy that you were assassinated. But, I expected you to provide the necessary leadership for change.

DR. KING

Resolving issues of race is too big a job for one man. I know that first hand.

RFK

This is very true, and it reminds me of something that I said: (He drifts into a contemplative moment.) *No matter what talent an individual possesses, what energy he might have, no matter how much integrity and how much honesty he might have, if he is by himself, and particularly a political figure, he can accomplish very little.* My brother had the support of the Democratic Party and had to gain more support for his efforts on Civil Rights. But first, he had to look after the country as a whole. The rest would not matter if he did not.

DR. KING

The president did eventually step up to the plate. But as Malcolm said, to the people suffering the day-to-day indignities of racism, any amount of time is like an eternity. *Wait means never.* And then once the president's earnest efforts did get underway, we all know what happened.

RFK

I worked under my brother's direction as attorney general, and there were, as he said, many other issues on our plate, such as fighting organized crime, which became a major undertaking. Nevertheless, my office worked on helping Blacks to vote and on integrating schools and public accommodations. It seems surreal that we went from that to having a Black presidential candidate forty years later. I always knew that this day would come sooner than later.

MALCOLM

Surreal would be a good word to describe it. This is no longer the America that I knew. Thank Heaven. It is coming closer to the America that I demanded.

RFK

It is neither the one that I knew, but for which I worked toward and for which many others sacrificed. I remember, so clearly, the Freedom Ride protestors. They were traveling across the U.S. by bus to protest the illegality of segregation. As attorney general I had to send special agent Siegenthaler to assist the demonstrators, and even he got caught in the fray and was injured. It turned out to be a bloody day for those brave young men and women.

DR. KING

For parents to watch their children being beaten and thrown in jail was the ultimate sacrifice.

RFK

I also remember in 1962 having to send U.S. marshals and troops to defend the first African American student to attend the University of Mississippi. James Meredith was a courageous young man because there were rioters and protestors that just wouldn't let up, and he had to learn in that environment. Jack and I worked on the Civil Rights Act of 1964. It passed under Lyndon Johnson.

MALCOLM

And you think that was enough, and you have the right to be here tonight—not with me you don't. (MALCOLM storms out of the door on the right.)

> (The three remaining men sit quietly, RFK and JFK on the couch and DR. KING in a chair.)

JFK

Maybe I shouldn't have come here this evening. It certainly did not turn out to be the joyous event I expected.

RFK

Don't doubt yourself now, big brother.

DR. KING

I don't think that you should be put off by Malcolm. When he puts the subject of race on the table for discussion, there is no sidestepping the issue because he doesn't mince words. I have come to respect him for that.

JFK

But, it is true. There was so much to do and so little time. The country needed to protect its national interests but also tend to its moral obligations if it was to remain a great nation that it was growing into.

RFK

I agree.

JFK

The country had to atone for some of its sordid history. A strategy for world peace definitely had to be put into place.

RFK

Still, you have a magnificent legacy, big brother. You signed the Nuclear Test Ban treaty and created the Peace Corps and the Alliance for Progress with Latin America. You got involved in the Civil Rights struggle and set the tone for others to follow in the path.

JFK

But, was it enough?

RFK

It was as much as you could do. That is one of the reasons I announced my candidacy for president of the United States. I had such strong feelings about what you had accomplished and what still needed to be done because of you, big brother. You did set the tenor for a new frontier, and I wanted to help shape it.

DR. KING

Mr. President, I remember a statement you made only a few months before your demise. You said: *We are confronted primarily with a moral issue. It is as old as the Scriptures and is as clear as the American Constitution. The heart of the question is whether all Americans are to be afforded equal rights and equal opportunities . . . Those who do nothing are inviting shame as well as violence. Those who do act boldly are recognizing right as well as reality.* Your heart was in the right place, and any doubt that I had has been removed.

JFK

Thank you, Dr. King, I had forgotten those remarks. However, those sentiments are engraved in my heart.

SCENE II

(The men have each separately paced back and forth to the radio several times while listening to and waiting for the latest results. Finally, they all sit sullenly on the couch, the brothers on opposite ends and DR. KING in the middle. Then the latest results are announced, and, at the same time, they are startled by a sudden slamming of the door on the left. MALCOLM has returned.)

MALCOLM
This is my night . . . . I shouldn't be the one leaving. (He nestles himself in one of the chairs.)

JFK
Maybe I should be the one to leave. (He rises.)

DR. KING
(He walks over to MALCOLM and pats him on the back and directs his comments to JFK.)

No, you shouldn't, sit. None of us should leave. Gentlemen, we all had similar goals, surely for the betterment of mankind. We used different methods and had dissimilar philosophies for achieving them. Brother Malcolm and I had a chance to acknowledge some of our divergent views when we met to plan today's event. After he and I talked for awhile, we decided that we wanted to share this special evening because we, in reality, had much in common and a vested interest in the outcome of the presidential race.

JFK
Yes, indeed, you two had different methods. (Glances guardedly at MALCOLM.) Malcolm's rhetoric during the 60's made you a pleasure to work with, Dr. King.

MALCOLM

Although my views shifted after my trip to Mecca, I still felt that protest and demonstrations were outdated. I didn't understand the point of it all. Black people were willing to be thrown into jail with little to no money to be bailed out. It seemed that those racist counties were making some easy money on court fees and bail bonds off the backs of suffering Black people. That didn't sit right with me. The judicial system was the new plantation.

DR. KING

It was unfortunate that young people had to be criminalized in order to acquire their rights. We had to raise funds just to pay bails. I would say by far that was the lowest point in the American jurist prudence system in that it did not stand up to protect Black citizens. It was structural criminality enhanced by a mob culture. A majority visited injustice on defenseless minorities with the courts standing on the sidelines. The jury system in the south aided and abetted the injustice.

MALCOLM

The police were out there wielding those clubs, bashing in the heads of innocent Black people, and all those Blacks ended up with were crushed, bloody skulls. Why some of those folks weren't good for anything else after that. Then there were the attack dogs ripping open the flesh of our people, and all they were expected to do was to turn the other cheek. And after turning the other cheek, they're supposed to love their oppressors. White folks couldn't understand why Black folks had bad things to say about them. It just didn't make sense, especially if a man is just trying to claim what is supposed to be his God given rights. Not to mention, the results didn't seem quite worth the effort. Progress moved at a piecemeal pace. I never believed in unjustified extremism but when *a human being is exercising extremism, in defense of liberty for human beings, it's no vice . . . Old Patrick Henry said liberty or death.* So I felt the revolutionary method would be much more effective.

JFK

Civil Disobedience has been used effectively throughout the world to effect change without violence. It takes a special talent to be able to use this method.

MALCOLM

If it's so effective, then why didn't the Founding Fathers use it? They petitioned, they redressed, but after awhile they got the message. It was time for a good old revolution, a good ole ass kickin'. As Frederick Douglass said, "power concedes nothing without struggle."

DR. KING

I believe there is a misconception about the use of civil disobedience. With non-violent resistance people do resist in a very strong and determined manner. It is not to be mistaken for non-resistance which is stagnant, passive and amounts to nothing more than complacency and do-nothingness.

MALCOLM

The point is that non-violence was being encouraged by the so-called liberal Whites at that time so that should make one just a little bit suspicious. White allies advised Blacks to utilize the non-violent method and to be patient and take beatings. What kind of allies are those? Yet, when it was time for them to stop their own oppression in the colonies, they called for revolution and still celebrate that revolution every 4th of July with great pride. *No, if we wanted some white allies, we needed the kind that John Brown was, or we didn't need them.*

DR. KING

Still, the non-violent movement was effective. It had a paralyzing effect on the power structure. The eyes of the world looked upon America and the Bull Connors of the world who turned dogs and water hoses on innocent, defenseless Black people, still being victimized by their oppressors after hundreds of years. What leadership could a country that treated it citizens this way provide for other nations, a country that denounced communism and the Holocaust but treated its Black citizens no better.

MALCOLM

So, Dr. King, you're saying that without world pressure, things would have not changed on its own in America? That says a lot about the moral culpability of White Americans at that time. Did you ever think that maybe Blacks were brought to America to civilize Whites, and not the other way around, like it's depicted in those shameless history books we were forced to read in order to brainwash us into docility?

DR. KING

That's certainly an intriguing concept, but I am not sure that I follow you, Malcolm.

MALCOLM

Let's examine this theory. Since Blacks have been in America there has been tremendous change in White Americans' morals and views: I think Blacks have helped tremendously to shape those views.

DR. KING

Go on.

RFK

Let me be clear before you proceed. You are saying, thus far, that Whites were the true heathens, and the Africans were the truly civilized group?

MALCOLM

Before we go any further, I want to be clear that I am not trying to make an indictment against White people because I've come too far for that type of petty retribution. However, if you start with the genocide of Native Americans, then look at the history and treatment of Blacks in this country and, then today, finally, there is a Black presidential candidate, that is dramatic change and growth of White people. No matter how harshly Blacks were treated, they never physically turned on Whites. I think Blacks have saved Whites. This was achieved mainly through unconditional love of White people by Black people. Black folks modeled true love and acceptance. Whites have gone from murdering and brutalizing people of color to electing them into office. Hey, White people even have a little bit of soul now. They're no longer so rigid and emotionless. (Laughs.)

DR. KING

Interesting concept, Malcolm, but you omit the positive things that Blacks have gained from Whites. I prefer to look at it as a relationship that has taught both groups many things. We have learned from each other.

JFK

All societies have evolved. The more we have achieved as a nation, the more we have of which to be proud. As a nation we will not allow the undoing of all of our great achievements. Each generation should find himself committed to the betterment of society.

RFK

As such, whether serving as attorney general, senator, or presidential candidate, I firmly committed myself to the twin ideals of freedom and social justice. It is the moral responsibility of each member of society to take action. Growth comes in this form. I stood against injustice, poverty, and prejudice, while cautioning others never to turn a blind eye. I was following in my brother's footsteps. Each of us here tonight was in our own way involved in the Civil Rights Movement to affect some type of positive change; it seems like yesterday.

JFK

You are right. It was only yesterday. I remember so clearly.

> (JFK stands up and walks over to the podium on the right, which has been serving as a book stand. For the moment he

is transposed to a different time when he
was giving a speech. He faces the audience
as the light becomes transfixed on him.)

*Robert Frost said it, Two roads diverged in a wood and I—/I took
the one less traveled by,/And that has made all the difference.*

(There is the sound of applause from a
fictitious audience. JFK turns slightly and
continues with a speech that evidently
occurred at a different venue)

*The world is very different now. For man holds in his mortal hands
the power to abolish all forms of human poverty and all forms
of human life. And yet the same revolutionary beliefs for which
our forebears fought are still at issue around the globe—the belief
that the rights of man come not from the generosity of the state
but from the hand of God.*

(Applause—JFK pauses briefly and then
begins again.)

*. . . In the long history of the world, only a few generations have
been granted the role of defending freedom in its hour of maximum
danger. I do not shrink from this responsibility—I welcome it. I do
not believe that any of us would exchange places with any other
people or any other generation. The energy, the faith, the devotion
which we bring to this endeavor will light our country and all who
serve it—and the glow from that fire can truly light the world.
And so, my fellow Americans: ask not what your country can do for
you—ask what you can do for your country.*

(Wild applause emanates from an audience
as JFK slowly returns to the present. The
light then becomes transfixed on the other
podium directly on the opposite side of the
room, on the left. There MALCOLM stands
as he did during a time in the 60's while

giving a speech to a warm, embracing audience.)

MALCOLM

The kind of demonstration you and I want and need is one that gets positive results. Not a one-day demonstration, but a demonstration until the end, the end of whatever we're demonstrating against. That's a demonstration. Don't say that you don't like what I did and you're going to come out and walk in front of my house for an hour. No, you're wasting your time. I'll sit down and go to sleep until your hour is up. If we're going to demonstrate, it should be a demonstration based upon no-holds barred.

(There is loud applause, and the light on MALCOLM dims and becomes transfixed on the podium on the right, where DR. KING is now standing.)

DR. KING
(DR. KING has draped his shoulders with a cloth that has been decorating the back of the couch. It is now a minister's shawl. He begins to address the audience. Music (the singer Odetta) from the civil rights era plays lightly in the background and applause is heard.)

Five score years ago, a great American, in whose symbolic shadow we stand, signed the Emancipation Proclamation. This momentous decree came as a great beacon light of hope to millions of Negro slaves who had been seared in the flames of withering injustice. It came as a joyous daybreak to end the long night of captivity.
But one hundred years later, we must face the tragic fact that the Negro is still sadly crippled by the manacles of segregation and the chains of discrimination

(Loud applause . . . the light dims on DR. KING and appears once again on MALCOLM

X, at the podium on the left, and he begins to speak.)

MALCOLM

We have to make the world see that the problem that we're confronted with is a problem for humanity . . . One of the first steps toward our being able to do this is to internationalize our problem. Let the world know that our problem is their problem. It's a problem for humanity. And the first form in which this can be done is the United Nations. One of the first acts of business of the Organization of Afro-American Unity is to organize the type of program that is necessary to take your and my case into the United Nations . . .

(Applause . . . the light dims on MALCOLM and appears once again on DR. KING, on the right, and he begins to speak. MAHALIA JACKSON is heard in the background saying, DR. KING, "tell them about the dream.")

DR. KING

I say to you today, my friends, that in spite of the difficulties and frustrations of the moment I still have a dream. It is deeply rooted in the American dream.

I have a dream that one day this nation will rise up and live out the true meaning of its creed: 'We hold these truths to be self-evident; that all men are created equal.'

I have a dream that one day on the red hills of Georgia the sons of former slaves and the sons of former slaveowners will be able to sit down together at the table of brotherhood . . . I have a dream today . . .

(Applause . . . the light dims, and then becomes transfixed on the opposite podium on the left. There stands RFK, at a time when he was giving a speech.)

RFK

I do not run for the presidency merely to oppose any man . . . I run to seek new policies—policies to end the bloodshed in Vietnam and in our cities. Policies to close the gaps that now exist between black and white, between rich and poor, between young and old. In this country and around the rest of the world . . .

> (Loud applause . . . the light dims on RFK briefly and reappears. He continues to speak.)

As a member of the cabinet and member of the Senate I have seen the inexcusable and ugly deprivation which causes children to starve in Mississippi, black citizens to riot in Watts; young Indians to commit suicide on their reservations because they've lacked all hope and they feel they have no future, and proud and able-bodied families to wait out their lives in empty idleness in eastern Kentucky.

> (The audience cheers. The lights readjust. The men are all standing shoulder-to-shoulder in the present; silently, they are reminiscing about the 60's.)

SCENE III

(The radio commentator is giving an analysis of the race. The men are all seated: MALCOLM and RFK on the couch and JFK and DR. KING in the chairs.)

DR. KING

The color of a man's skin doesn't matter. We know that now. In the end we all did what he could do with what was available and with what God gave us. Which candidate wins tonight will have to deal with the current issues facing America.

JFK

As much as things have changed, there are many things that remain the same. Hate groups continue to increase. Racism and discrimination are still apparent.

(The radio announcer says that other results have come in. The announcer says that Iowa has gone to Obama and West Virginia to McCain.)

JFK

Oh my goodness, I didn't even win in Iowa. What do you make of that?

RFK

I don't know how this is going to turn out, big brother, but Obama has a slight lead, so far. Some of the states were predictable. The people in those states have pretty much been set in their ways for a while now. It's the battleground states that we have to keep our eyes on tonight. I thought the race would be close. What's that, another state?

(The announcer comes in again. Wisconsin has gone to Obama and Kansas to his McCain.)

JFK

Really, I didn't win in Wisconsin. Things are really beginning to heat up. A Black man may truly be elected tonight.

DR. KING

This is beginning to become a real possibility. What do you think it will mean to have a Black president? If this truly happens, what will it mean for the country?

RFK

First off, the word black should be removed from the title, President. Yeah, sure, it will go down in the history books as the election of a first black president, but that adjective does not need to be a part of the day-to-day workings of the office. I think we will begin to have the makings of a color-blind society. This is the top office in the land and that means everything.

MALCOLM

In the past when a Black man was elected into office, a prized office like that of the mayor or governor, it was usually because the town or state had hit rock bottom, economically or otherwise, and it couldn't go any lower, so it was time to let a Black man run the system, cause he couldn't do any more damage than already had been done by his White predecessor, who was usually an incompetent White man. Plus, if the Black candidate was not able to turn things around, he took the blame for the state of affairs. In this instance, the country has had a tumultuous eight years with the Republican Party, and the country's in the toilet. Obama is in the right place at the appropriate time. If America was doing well, low unemployment, no wars, or international perils, Obama wouldn't be able to get his hands on this.

DR. KING

Maybe that's how it used to be, but I have to believe that real change is taking place for Obama to have come this far. From everything that we have heard about this man, he's got the goods. He's no standby or fly by night, in the right place at the right time kind of guy. He is the genuine article.

JFK

He also has a lot of credible people standing behind him, some of the old-time politicians as well. People don't put their careers on the line for just anybody, so I have to agree with you, Dr. King. There has been a paradigm shift in the country. We are looking at the future, a new era.

DR. KING

This would certainly be a major shift for the country. What do you think the implications will be? If the country wakes up tomorrow, and there is a Black president, how will things be different with regard to race?

JFK

I mentioned before that some things don't change. If he's elected, he'll have those who support him and a decent amount of people who will not. No doubt the Republicans will be looking ahead to the next election, so their main agenda will be how to discredit him or throw him off of his game and that won't have anything to do with race. It's just the nature of the two parties, and it's important to have two parties to keep everyone as honest as it is possible to be in the business of politics.

MALCOLM

You said that there will be a decent amount of people who will not support him, and some of those individuals will be racists. This group will not magically disappear into thin air. There will remain pockets of serious racists.

RFK

His election would actually help with race relations to some degree. Little Black boys and girls will have a magnificent role model and be inspired. They will believe that they can achieve the same dreams and become president. We know that in many of the inner cities, the communities are devoid of hope and without that the motivation to succeed is just not there.

JFK

Yes, there will be the belief of equality. Black people will have a sense that other Americans will regard them as equal. Black Americans will know that Whites could have voted differently, against Obama and for a White candidate who was also qualified, who was an American hero. This would be a voluntary action on the part of Whites, to vote for a Black man.

RFK

Exactly—White people would be sending a message loud and clear. Why was it important to vote against an American war hero for a Black man? This would be a clear message from White people that the country has changed.

JFK

It is not a challenge to White Americans. It is an evolution of White Americans. The young generation is going into a different direction than their ancestors. The young are leading the older generation in progressive thinking. They are tired of carrying around all of that excess baggage and guilt from the past.

MALCOLM

I would be a bit more cautious in my thinking. Such efforts as Affirmative Action will still be needed, but I believe that the argument to defend it will have to be retooled. It will cut across class lines to include poor people, the impoverished of all races. This may lead to conflict among classes of Blacks as well.

DR. KING

By your definition, this will change the term of victimology for Blacks.

MALCOLM

I would say so. Victimology would have to be redefined. It will go from oppression to denial of opportunities or preparation and will be more of a class issue, another war that will have to be waged.

JFK

This shift seems to have caught everyone off guard. The country changed so dramatically in such a short time that no one could have predicted it.

DR. KING

Just like when slavery had to end, people came together and abolished it, Black and White people. It is in the same way that White people fought a war to end slavery. The country was ready then for significant moral change, and I think it is ready now.

JFK

If Obama is elected president, the country will be forever changed. It will have come full circle.

RFK

I believe the rest will fall into place, but I am not so naïve as to think that this will happen all on its own. Continued dialogue will be needed, as well as more discussion and awareness. There will be a tendency for some people to cling to some of the old ways of thinking and acting. A coalition for continued change and growth will also be needed to forge continued progress. It will no longer be a Black movement. It will belong to everyone.

JFK

I have every confidence that the country can rise to the occasion.

MALCOLM
I believe the slogan is "Yes we can!" (They all laugh.)

DR. KING
Black people will have to grow and evolve with this movement. We talked about how restored hope will become an essential component for them. Another important element for uplift would be pride. Black people have truly never felt validated in this country. Why I knew a few people who refused to ever put up a flag on the 4th of July or any other holiday because they felt like second-class citizens. I bet more Black people would hang up flags and be able to feel like authentic Americans if Obama is elected. It is difficult growing up in a country where one is a citizen, but one does not have the privileges that other citizens enjoy. One doesn't get the first selections at anything, jobs, housing, and so on. One can taste it with his eyes but never in the truest sense. The election of a Black president will be empowering for Black people's pride and dignity.

MALCOLM
I agree with you. An election of a Black president will add a tremendous boost to hope and pride for Black folks. But the election of a Black man will not change people's minds and attitudes over night because racism includes Black men dying every day in the inner cities. Racism includes higher incarceration rates for Blacks.

DR. KING
An election of a Black president should mean an end to White domination over Blacks. For the Black man, someone else has always had to be in control of his life. He has been dependent on the goodness and mercy of White men, as if he were a child. They have controlled what he learned, what job he did, and where he lived. It is time for the Black man to create his own path. Self-determination, self-development, and self-respect will increase among Blacks.

(The conversation is interrupted with the announcement of Florida going to Obama.)

JFK

(Chuckles to himself.) That's another state that I didn't win. You never forget each state you won and each state you didn't win. I am finding this quite amusing, so forgive me, fellows.

(JFK walks over to the radio in a solemn moment.)

DR. KING

Do you think we can influence this race with a bit of prayer?

JFK

We can certainly give it a try.

MALCOLM

I'm game.

RFK

Let us pray for the Democrats. (The men come together in a circle to pray.)

ACT THREE

SCENE I

> (The four men are seated on the sofa and chairs—all captured in deep thought. JFK and DR. KING are seated on the couch and MALCOLM AND RFK in the two chairs opposite one another. The radio is giving an update on the recent states the candidates have won. Obama has just gained Colorado and New Mexico and appears to be leading, but it is too soon to call. The four men are amazed at the results. JFK is first to break the silence as he stands up and walks over to the radio and stares at it in amazement.)

> JFK
> (He walks in front of the couch to address the men who are still seated.)

Gentlemen, the course of history will be changed tonight, regardless of who wins. Even if the new vice president is a woman, it will provide a new landscape for this country. I have to allow for a few regrets now that the race is getting so close. I intended to do more for Civil Rights, and then I would be an even bigger part of this moment.

> MALCOLM

That's what I've been saying. You should have done more. (Throws his hands up in the air.)

> DR. KING

You could not be more a part of this moment than you are right now, Mr. President. This is your moment, too.

JFK
I was just standing here thinking how a moral act can be so unpopular among so many? Alas, it was not meant to be.

MALCOLM
A moral act can be wrong because people tend to see what they want to see. A stereotype is a hard thing to break down. For example, stereotypes about Black people started during slavery, and so many of them have since been disproven, but people continue to interpret situations in the same way.

RFK
That's a strange thing. Why do you think that is so?

MALCOLM
Some people get things fixed in their minds and keep it that way even if the evidence speaks to the contrary because they feel comfortable holding on to what's familiar and what they can count on. Black people have proven themselves in so many ways, lawyers, doctors, athletes, but the script takes so long to be rewritten when Blacks present positive attributes. And one instance of failure will be used to stereotype the whole group very quickly. One Black man robs a bank and all of a sudden all Black people are thieves and degenerates. White men can commit all types of crimes from serial killings to drug deals, but his crimes are never visited on White people as a whole. Each Black person carries the whole race of his people on his back in this way. That's one thing I hope will change if Obama wins this election.

DR. KING
There has to be a vested interest to hold onto a stereotype after it has been disproven so many times. It is about greed and power. It has been that way from day one for Blacks. The wealth that the slave trade brought to this country was incalculable. Letting go of these beliefs means sharing the power that has been concentrated in the hands of the privileged group for centuries.

RFK

Interesting . . . . (Nodding to DR KING'S comments.) Jack, back to your original comment, you have no reason to have even the littlest of regrets. You accomplished a lot, and you were on the verge of making great change when you were taken away.

DR. KING

Tell us about that day, Mr. President. Did you have any idea that something like that was about to happen to you? Did you know that you would be taken away so suddenly?

JFK

I did not foresee that fateful day. It was a sunny day. (He walks toward the radio, lost in thought.) Actually, it was a Friday afternoon on November 22, 1963 in Dallas, Texas, as Jacqueline and I rode along in the motorcade in the back seat of the convertible through Dealey Plaza, waving to the crowd.

> (JFK waves his arm in the air and smiles broadly as if back in that moment.)

We were so happy and life was good. I had my work and the many challenges that came with it. I had some aches and pains from the war. While I was in the navy, our ship was rammed by a Japanese destroyer, but I was dealing with that. I loved my wife, children, and my country. I was just basking in the glory of being a larger part of this great country.

> (He stops waving and reluctantly puts his arm down, and a fearful look appears on his face.)

That's when it happened. I was hit in my head and throat. My part was done, right then, no more, no less. I had so many plans to make America better, but when a thing is done, it is done! Sure, if I knew it would be the last moment, I would do things differently, cram in as much of the good stuff as I could, but it was not for me to finish. My part was done and set aside. There were other dramatis personae in the plan, God's plan.

RFK

Jack, there is no need for you to harbor any regrets whatsoever. You are a wonderful brother, and you were a wonderful president. That's why I wanted to follow in your footsteps, become president and continue to work on some of those important issues you started in on. A new day was dawning! (RFK goes over and lays a hand on his brother's shoulder.)

JFK

No, Bobby, I do know better and that regrets are just another road that could have been taken, and all roads can lead to regrets. Don't you see? It's just that in the grand scheme of things, you don't always realize your part. You don't always follow your intuitions and insights. You can't always know what is real or what you might be imagining. There are always so many things, distractions and everything seems as if it's so important. So, you try to attend to everything because you are not sure what will really matter the most. Sometimes you have to make your mark in a limited area. I was just coming into that, coming into knowing and being the kind of president that would make people real proud. I knew my next steps and was anxious and enthused about taking them.

MALCOLM

I know exactly what you mean about being enthused and then being shut down. (Goes over to JFK and gives his shoulder a quick squeeze.)

JFK

(Looks at MALCOLM, acknowledging his support.) My part was over before I felt it had even begun. Not being able to raise my children was my greatest disappointment, but they turned out fine. I think we all had that in common, being separated from our young children.

RFK

You were sorely missed, big brother. The nation was stunned and confused. At first it was thought that there was an attack on the nation since we were in the middle of the cold war. Lyndon Johnson was just two cars behind you, and people wanted to know if he was safe. The country was in an absolute state of shock. People were weeping in the streets. Some gathered together in department stores to watch the news. Many were praying that the news wasn't true. Everything came to a standstill. World leaders expressed their shock that something like this would happen in the United States.

DR. KING

It was, undeniably, a travesty, Mr. President. When you were assassinated, it was a clear sign to me that I was not safe in this kind of a world, when a president who was so beloved could be gunned down that way. I think that's something that we all have in common. We were all just on the verge . . . .

JFK

Dr. King, maybe you are right and that's why we all ended up here together this evening.

> (JFK and RFK return to their seats. Another state is announced on the radio in Obama's favor, Washington. MALCOLM X goes over to the radio and lays his left hand on it while placing his right hand flat against his chest, bowing his head and shutting his eyes in an introspective moment. After a few moments, he turns to address JFK.)

MALCOLM

Mr. President, I really do know what you mean. I thought that I was supposed to do it all, save my people, deliver them, like Moses, to the Promised Land. I had a passion that was like a fire in my belly that couldn't be extinguished. I had to just act on it. I could see everything so clearly, like a revelation. It all came to me, especially after my trip to Mecca. I no longer had any control over my actions because I was on God's mission. I was an instrument, but I thought I was supposed to do it all, finish what I started. How could I be given a gift to help my people and not be allowed to carry out the plans to save them? I saw the shortcomings of the races.

RFK

Tell us more about the revelation? What else did you see lying ahead?

MALCOLM

It was like I had been living in the darkness all of my young life. Even though I was ignorant, everything that happened to me, the foster home, drugs, prison, everything was to prepare me to accept my vision, the truth. The events that I lived through allowed me to accept my predestined role.

RFK

How did you come to acceptance of what you needed to do?

MALCOLM

Like the President just said, the truth is not easy to recognize even in the broad daylight of the mind. Truth is strewn there among so many other things that occupy our thoughts, among the clutter and doubt. Only when it is set against the backdrop of a harsh and ugly reality can one begin to recognize it, when one begins to search for the meaning of such suffering and pain. I had to transverse the deepest and darkest echelons of society to recognize what was right there in front of me all along. Without those experiences, I would not have accepted my role in the struggle.

DR. KING

Yes, Brother Malcolm, you had to allow yourself to see the truth and then not to be afraid because it was unknown and alien. It is like finding a treasure buried among the ruins that you were not expecting to find. Once found, fear cannot even keep you from what you know you must do with it. The truth is the only thing that can sometimes set you free.

MALCOLM

Fear becomes the least concern because then it is all out of your control. Once you find the truth, the passion comes on its own, and there is no turning around. Certainly, you are aware of the implications of your actions when you stand up for what you believe, but it is a runaway train at that point.

JFK

You are aware of the risks, but they are minor in the larger scheme of things. I believe each man is placed on earth with a task set before him. Did you know that it was your time, Malcolm?

MALCOLM

Unlike you, Mr. President, I lived under constant threat of death. I began each day knowing that it might be my last, and I could just hope for enough time to make my message clearer and put a plan in motion that would help my people. I did think that I had been given a wonderful gift, and it would not be wasted by my premature death.

RFK

I certainly understand what you are saying. Tell us how it happened?

MALCOLM

It was the 21st day of February 1965, and I was at the Audubon Ballroom in Manhattan. I was launching my new organization, the Organization of Afro-American Unity. I was optimistic about the new direction in which I would be leading my people.

JFK

What direction was this?

MALCOLM

This was shortly after the trip to Mecca where I had gained a new perspective on race. I was no longer preaching the separatist philosophy for Blacks. I wanted to work with the other Civil Rights leaders, if possible, to internationalize the plight of Blacks in America. I saw that the issue of race in the country was going to be a major undertaking, and needed to be brought before the United Nations.

JFK

Did you know that it might happen on that day?

MALCOLM

Well, as I said, I was on borrowed time. I was already dead. Every day was a gift. My life had come full circle. There were dangers I had tried to escape when I was a drug dealer and pimp that I was facing once again. I was being hunted down like an animal in the streets.

RFK

How did this make you feel?

MALCOLM

I was just so tired of running, trying to avoid the inevitable.

DR. KING

Tell us what happened next.

MALCOLM

(Begins with a faraway look.) That day at the Audubon Ballroom was the first meeting of the OAAU. I had given orders to my people that they shouldn't search anyone at the door as they arrived. I don't really know why. Perhaps I didn't want to discourage new members. Even now it doesn't make sense that I didn't take more precaution. I didn't actually believe that it would happen that day, especially with my pregnant wife and four daughters sitting in the front row. I felt that I had a mission and would at least be able to put the plans for the new organization into action. It wasn't egotism, but I thought I was special because I had been given a gift. The blinders were off. Everything that I had to do was so clear. But that's just when it happened.

JFK

Go on, Malcolm.

MALCOLM

There was a commotion in the audience.

>(MALCOLM is mentally taken back to a painful place as a look of terror emerges on his face.)

Immediately, I sensed danger. My body tensed almost at the same time that it was riddled with many bullets while I stood there speaking, and my message was stopped in mid-sentence. (Becoming reanimated with a sigh of relief.) But I have this to say: you can kill the messenger, but you cannot kill the message. My message has lived on to ring true in many people's ears around the world. I had to die for people to hear my message. I realize that now. At that time many people, both Black and White were not prepared to hear the truth about race relations because it was so ugly and foreign. They could not look deeply into the mirror that I held up and recognize themselves. But eventually they understood. I became a symbol.

>(DR. KING goes to MALCOLM and embraces him. Both men hug and pat each other's back. The radio cuts in. Nevada has gone to Obama. They both stare at the radio and embrace once more. MALCOLM goes to sit down on the couch next to JFK. DR. KING stands over the radio, head bowed as if in prayer over the latest results.)

DR. KING

It was a difficult time for many people, Malcolm. I sent a telegram to Sister Betty expressing my sadness. Although it may not have been publicly known, I always had a deep affection for you. I thought you were an eloquent spokesmen.

RFK

I remember people having mixed feelings. Those who knew of your value to the Black liberation movement were devastated. Those who were caught up in the misconceptions of your life would soon learn for what you stood.

DR. KING

(Looks at the radio.) Gentlemen, it doesn't appear that this will be a long election evening the way these results are coming in. (Looks toward MALCOLM.) Brother Malcolm, I agree that although you may know that there is a strong probability that your life will be cut short because the actions that you have decided to take are frowned upon by some of the majority in power, it's not knowing if or when. You are right that sometimes you become hopeful that you might be able to complete your work. Many deemed your message and delivery harsher than mine. At some point they were forced to deal with me, so they wouldn't have to deal with you. But that didn't make them like me any more than you.

RFK

That was a proud moment when you were presented with the Nobel Prize, Dr King.

DR. KING

Yes, but in the end it did not matter to those who sought to silence me; I never understood how a non-violent protest could bring out the worst in some White Americans. I was only seeking peace. Why, I was awarded the Nobel Peace Prize, which some would think should sanction my actions to work for peace and fairness, if only it were that simple.

RFK

I thought about my brother so much the day you were assassinated, Dr. King.

JFK

Did you, Bobby? It seemed as though those were dangerous times, whether you were White or Black.

DR. KING

It was April 4, 1968, another sunny day, and I was feeling very positive about the Southern Christian Leadership's purpose for being in Memphis. I was with Ralph Abernathy, Andrew Young, Jesse Jackson, James Bevel and Samuel Kyles and some others. We had gone to Memphis to support the black garbage workers of local 1733. We had already been there the month before and had a rally. Then we returned a short time later for a protest march which erupted in violence. A young man was shot and killed. I was disheartened that the violence took place.

MALCOLM

Why disheartened? Weren't Black people being physically attacked during the marches?

DR. KING

Yes, they were. But at the heart of every non-violent campaign is the appeal to the *conscience of the local and national community*. We have to be able to accept blows without retaliation. So there was unfinished business in Memphis. We needed to return and try to get it right this time.

RFK

I understood that you were actually working on another march at the time and Memphis was not really planned. Was it fate that took you back to that place?

DR. KING

Yes, actually it was fate that pulled me in that direction. We had to tend to the needs of the people in Memphis. At that time, the SCLC was working on a poor people's march on poverty in Washington D. C. Andrew Young thought that we should stay focused on that. But something pulled me in the direction of Memphis. I didn't feel that we had done justice or for that matter gotten any justice the last time we were there.

MALCOLM
Dr. King, it didn't matter if it was Memphis or somewhere else, you know?

DR. KING
Yes, I know that. Yet, the Black sanitation workers were being treated unfairly, and it was reason enough to return and support their earlier efforts. They were making much less per hour than the White workers and when it rained, they would not be paid, but the White workers did. Worse, violence was being used against them. I knew we could not give our attention to every unfair cause, but it was the sense of justice that pulled us in the direction of Memphis.

JFK
How do you recall the events of that fateful day?

DR. KING
The day before I had spoken to an audience that included the Black sanitation workers. I gave my "Mountain Top" speech as I called it. I gave that speech during what I thought were the most dangerous times. Funny, I didn't think of this trip as one of those times. I had, though, been feeling off that week, rather bleak and tired. I had been going strong since 1955 with the bus boycott and knew I needed to eventually take a little break from the movement. I knew my family could use some time. They sacrificed a lot for the movement. Anyway, I gave my "Mountain Top" speech.

(He mimics part of the speech as if revisiting that time.)

I might not get there with you . . . . Actually, I knew this day was going to come. Ever since that incident in the department store, I carried this feeling, like a foreshadowing.

JFK
The department store?

DR. KING
Yes, it was in 1963. I was in a Harlem department store signing autographed copies of my book, *Stride Toward Freedom*. As I was signing my name to the page, I felt a sharp pain in my chest. I couldn't quite figure out why I was having this pain. But it turns out a woman had taken it upon herself to stab me with a letter opener. Afterwards, she stood there cool, calm, and quite pleased with herself. She was a good example of a person with a strong aversion to change. The hatred she must have felt for me that day for her to try and kill me like some animal. I nearly died as the tip of the opener rested on my aorta. Surgery saved me, but I never forgot that day and carried it with me as a reminder that I might not have much time to complete my work.

RFK
And that fateful day came in Memphis.

DR. KING
Yes, it did. The group of us was staying at the Lorraine Motel. We had been invited to Reverend Kyles' house for dinner. Andrew, Jesse and James were in the parking lot, and Sam was out on his balcony next door. I was leaning over the balcony talking to some of the others in the courtyard while waiting for Ralph. The work we were doing was difficult. Behind each event, it took multiple meetings and planning, and along with that came a lot of uncertainty. We were, however, deeply committed to the non-violent message. I was about to turn and leave the balcony when the shot rang out, right in my neck through the tip of my chin. I didn't know what had hit me, just slumped to the floor.

(DR. KING falls silent, slumping forward while still standing, and JFK goes over to him and puts a firm hand on his shoulder and leads him to a seat on the couch next to MALCOLM X.)

RFK

I do remember that fateful day, Dr King. It was horrific, shocking, and unexpected. I was scheduled to speak at a campaign rally in Indianapolis on that day. When I arrived, I was given the sad news. The police advised me against making the campaign stop because it was in the heart of the ghetto. When I arrived, the people were upbeat, only because they didn't know about your assassination yet. I had to be the one to break the news to them.

MALCOLM

I bet that went over well.

RFK

It was a difficult thing to do. I wasn't hesitant, though, because I was caught up in the sadness of such a senseless act. Sometimes one's faith in humanity wavers, but one has to believe in the goodness of man. I know that's how Dr. King would have felt at that moment. So, I tried to take my cue from what he might do. And, if I planned to be a president for all the people, I had to be able to speak to all the people.

MALCOLM

You had to be taking your life into your own hands with that because as I understand it, the whole country was rioting after Dr. King was assassinated. In the days that followed in over a hundred cities, rioting, fire-bombings, sniper firings, and then the federal troops were called out. That is what I have heard took place.

RFK

Surely, it was a delicate matter. Dr. King was loved by many people. I started off by telling the crowd that Dr. King stood for non-violence and that he *dedicated his life to love and justice between fellow human beings.*

MALCOLM

Then what happened? How could you keep a crowd like that under control under those circumstances?

RFK

I continued on and the crowd began to listen. I told them: *For those of you who are black—considering the evidence is that there were white people who were responsible—you can be filled with bitterness, and with hatred, and a desire for revenge.* Basically I asked them if that was the direction they wanted the country to move in, more polarization and hatred or the direction that Dr. King had charted out, toward understanding and compassion. I told them that I understood their pain because I, too, had lost a loved one to violence, a member of my family, who was also killed by a White man. (Looks at JFK.)

MALCOLM

They would have to sympathize with you on that one. An assassination of a loved one is a hard thing to live through, let alone forget.

RFK

Yes, the crowd related the loss of a beloved president with the loss of Dr. King. I told the crowd that we did not need any more division, lawlessness, violence, and hatred. We needed love, wisdom, and compassion, whether we are White or Black. Those were my true sentiments and also Dr. King's beliefs. And I missed my brother so much at that moment. So I continued and said to the crowd: *The vast majority of white people and the vast majority of black people in this country want to live together, want to improve the quality of our life, and want justice for all human beings that abide in our land.* I was interrupted by applause. But it was still such a sad, sad day.

DR. KING
I think that is true, what you just said, Senator. The vast majority of White and Black people want to live together in peace. That's why Obama is leading in this election.

MALCOLM
It took an awfully long time from the time you gave that speech, Senator, to people coming to that realization now, of living together in peace.

JFK
Bobby, did you have any idea at that time that your own demise was only months away? Here you are giving this wonderful speech to the people, and in a few months, the violence would be turned on you. All of these assassinations are truly unbelievable.

RFK
Yes, it was unbelievable. Sure, Dr. King's untimely demise was truly shocking and appalling. Still, I was on the verge of something wonderful. I was campaigning for the presidential nomination to carry on your good work, Jack. But, I intended to help carry out Dr. King's dream once I got elected and into the White House. I had a vision for our country to make things better, a vision that you started, big brother. I had no time to think about the danger that might be involved.

> (RFK looks affectionately at JFK and walks over to the radio although no results are coming in at the moment.)

At that point, it was all the more important to stay strong and continue forward toward the presidency.

JFK

It was just two months later that you were gunned down. How could that happen? I still could not get over this happening to two brothers in the same family. It was difficult enough when we lost our eldest brother, Joe, when his plane was shot down in WWII.

RFK

I don't know how it could have happened either. Was it truly a reflection of the climate of the country that we lived in? Did I underestimate the evil that existed? I guess I should have seen how dangerous the times were with all of these assassinations taking place in the 60's. I didn't think someone would kill another Kennedy in the same way. Nor did I think that someone would be so heartless to take away another member of the same family, allowing so many children to be left fatherless. Terrorism had its grip on the times then.

MALCOLM

Terrorism has existed in this country since its founding. It is time to clean house.

DR. KING

Evil is in existence at all times. All men, and women, for that matter, have inherent evil tendencies. They have to choose between the good and the evil that exist within. There comes a critical time in one's life when one has to choose.

MALCOLM

Do you simply believe that it is a matter of choice for some people?

DR. KING

Yes, to a large degree this is the case although I believe that some people are born with the tendency to do good, in the same way that some men are born evil. But they always have the opportunity to choose and change. It's not always easy, but they have the choice.

JFK

Dr. King, why do you suppose that some men choose evil over goodness?

DR. KING

They make the mistake of succumbing blindly and wholeheartedly to at least one of the seven deadly sins. That is the measure upon which men will be judged. However, when one is susceptible to corruption, it's usually over power. They equate power with control over others, like Hitler. Or, they equate wealth with the ability to buy power over others.

RFK

That has been the downside to America's promise, power and corruption, along with self-delusion in order to justify bad choices.

DR. KING

Yes, there is power in being able to discriminate against others in order to dictate their circumstances. In the process people become ruthless and give into greed, ill-gotten gains. For some it is a very thin line. They will go back and forth between good and evil. One day committing evil deeds, and the next day trying to make up for them by doing good, but it never balances out because the pain and suffering they cause cannot be undone. Only total contrition overrides mortal sins; that is a true test of a changed heart.

MALCOLM

This typified the society we lived in, wolves in sheep's clothing. I didn't even know who to trust anymore.

DR. KING

I do believe, though, that man is inherently good. It is the temptations to do evil that clouds the judgment, but all evils are related in some way to the seven deadly sins. It is up to man to practice the contrasting values associated with these sins.

MALCOLM

That's good advice—to practice the contrasting virtues of Pride, Greed, Envy, Wrath, Lust, Gluttony, and Sloth—interesting analysis, Dr. King.

JFK

It is very much so, but please, Bobby, continue. I believe you were at one of your highest points, celebrating the victory of the California primary.

RFK

Yes, I was in Los Angeles, California, celebrating the successful campaign in the primary there. It was two months after Dr. King departed; it was just after midnight on June 5, 1968. I had addressed my supporters in the Ambassador Hotel's Embassy Ballroom and was on my way to a press conference, which never took place. My aides and security said we would cut through the Kitchen and pantry area behind the ballroom to the press area. On the way I was hemmed in by the crowd, joyously shaking hands along the way, when it happened.

JFK

You were riding high with a sense of victory at that moment, weren't you?

RFK

Very much so . . . .

> (RFK's face is suddenly frozen in pain as he recounts the events of that day.)

Then a guy steps out from a tray stacker beside the ice machine and begins to repeatedly fire shots from a 22-caliber. A pregnant Ethel was at my side. (Returns slowly to the present.) You ever notice how time slows down during those moments even though you are powerless to stop what is happening? As a result, I was given a few extra moments to reflect on my life. I barely survived the three-hour surgery . . . . to no avail.

(DR. KING and JFK go to RFK's side, and each places a reassuring hand on each of his shoulders. MALCOLM joins them in a solemn moment.)

MALCOLM

I've been thinking. There's something else we all have in common, other than all being assassinated in the sixties and standing up for Civil Rights. There are also all of those conspiracy theories connected to our deaths and . . . .

(MALCOLM is unable to finish his thought because at that moment someone knocks on the door while also pushing it open. A tall, bearded man appears in the doorway on the right. He has a slight smile and is wearing a top hat. Everyone is startled as they view the VISITOR.)

VISITOR

(The VISTOR steps into the room and sizes up the four men, who are all very obviously stunned into silence.)

Well, isn't this delightful. (Looking around.) I heard only a few hours ago that you all were here waiting for the election results. I am afraid that I am late, but once I heard this news, I wanted to come immediately and be with you. Have all the results come in? I hope I am not too late.

JFK

Not yet, sir. So far, your being here is the biggest surprise of the evening and will remain so unless, of course, Obama wins.

VISITOR

I hope I am not intruding or creating a disruption of the unfolding events.

JFK

I think once we all get over the initial shock that we all would be honored to have you here with us. But, tell me, why are you here?

RFK

Yes, I am rather curious myself as to what brings you here.

DR. KING

Indeed, I am still rather stunned. But I would like to know, too.

MALCOLM

Yes, I am rarely speechless, but this is the second time this evening that I seem to be at a loss for words.

VISITOR

When I heard that you all had the extraordinary idea to end up here together to wait out the election results, I didn't give it another thought. And here I am. I knew that I had to come and be able to share this auspicious occasion with you, gentlemen. I thought it would truly be most fitting. Now that I am here, I feel as if my heart is about to burst with joy. It feels like Heaven. (The men all look at one another.)

MALCOLM

This night has been one full of surprises for me. When I agreed to meet Dr. King here to wait for the election results, I never imagined anything like this happening. First, these handsome brothers show up. (Referencing JFK and RFK.) Now you show up. If this don't beat all! I am as puzzled now as I was when I first saw them as to reason you want to be here for the election results? Why was it so important for you to be part of this crowd?

VISITOR

Why wouldn't I want to be here? I am very hopeful about this Democratic candidate.

RFK

That's delightful news, coming from a Republican, but I think you were a very moderate one at that.

MALCOLM

The reason you are here may be obvious to everyone else, but it's not to me.

VISITOR

Malcolm, let me guess. You didn't think much of my intentions and actions when I had the chance to make a difference in race relations. Is that why you are questioning my motives?

MALCOLM

Yes, actually I don't think you did enough. What I mean is that I don't think your actions were purposeful. It's not like you had any intentions of freeing slaves, so they could run for president.

VISITOR

All I can say in my defense is that things are not always as they seem. I won't blame any of my shortcomings on being a product of the times from which I came, although that is partly true. It is hard to reinterpret or reinvent a society that you are born into. A practice that is a way of life appears normal. The indoctrination that one is given solidifies the whole of it. But no matter what, one begins to form his or her own opinions of what is right and wrong and that is what I eventually did.

MALCOLM

Are you saying that you did not know that slavery was wrong?

VISITOR

It is true. I was conflicted about the Black race for much of my life. I knew slavery was wrong, finally, at some point.

MALCOLM

You know I have studied your works well, and I remember some of the ideas that you had. Remember what you said in that speech you gave in 1858 in Charleston: *I will say, then, that, I am not nor ever been, in favor of bringing about in any way the social and political equality of the white and black races . . .*

(MALCOLM's quote is interrupted by the VISITOR.)

VISITOR

I remember those words all too well.

(The VISITOR continues the speech where MALCOLM left off.)

. . . that I am not, nor ever have been, in favor of making voters or jurors of Negroes, nor of qualifying them to hold office, nor to intermarry with white people: and I will say in addition to this, that there is a physical difference between the white and black races which I believe will forever forbid the two races living together on terms of social and political equality. And inasmuch as they cannot so live, while they do remain together there must be in the position of superior and inferior, and I, as much as any other man, am in favor of having the superior position assigned to the white race.

MALCOLM

Well, do you know why we are gathered here tonight?

VISITOR

I do. A Black man might be elected president.

MALCOLM

How do you explain those words you uttered so long ago? Those words would make it seem contrary for you to come here this evening, unless you came here to try and jinx the election.

DR. KING

Obviously, you have had a change of heart since then.

VISITOR

Well, that was in 1858, and I had much to learn in the next few years, just like you all would in your life time. At that point I knew slaves had to be free, much beyond that I hadn't figured it out. I could not even wrestle with the question of equality when many in our nation were much opposed to freedom alone.

JFK

All of this sounds very familiar. I went through something like this, wresting with the unpopular issue of race.

VISITOR

Yes, that's what led to my defeat in my bid for U.S. Senate in 1858, the issue of race.

JFK

You are referring to the "House Divided" speech, no doubt that you gave at the Republican Convention. History has already told us a great deal about you. No one can say that you did not stand on principle. You believed that the Supreme Court ruling on the Dred Scott case was part of a larger conspiracy to turn all of the free states back into slave states, didn't you?

VISITOR

The Dred Scott case and the Nebraska Act were part of a conspiratorial plan because the two worked hand-in-hand. They were intended to make people indifferent to slavery; they could vote it up or down. Congress had no authority to prohibit slavery. *Certainly the people of a State are and ought to be subject to the Constitution of the United States.* The Dred Scott ruling would diminish the freedom that freed slaves had acquired in the North because they had no protection under the Constitution.

RFK

The country was still so new, still developing and growing. States were sovereign. The Union was more of a voluntary compact at that time. A strong central government had not been developed.

Up until that point it had been a myriad of compromises that kept the South and the North together.

VISITOR

Yes, and one of my most important missions was not to allow the dissolution of the Union. The preservation of a unified nation and a new birth of freedom were my twin goals.

DR. KING

You did not have any real solutions for Black people at that time.

VISITOR

I did give some thought to colonization. In 1862 when I issued the Emancipation Proclamation, I was working out a plan to ship freed slaves to Haiti or Liberia. In my heart I knew it would seem like we had used a group of people for labor for hundreds of years and then decided to throw them out like too-soiled cloth.

MALCOLM

What happened to that plan? Another dead end as far as Black people were concerned.

VISITOR

Then, as I was drafting the Emancipation Proclamation as a first step, I became desperate. The war had been going on for a while, and the Union army needed the help of slaves. I didn't much trust that slaves would be capable of fighting in the Civil War, but at that point, I had no choice and included a provision in the Emancipation Proclamation for them to be equipped to fight for the Union.

DR. KING

As history has written it, you were pleasantly surprised by your decision, which was based largely on your need to save the Union.

VISITOR

Yes, freed men and slaves enlisted in droves. The eagerness of slaves to fight for their own freedom began to turn my thoughts around considerably about this race of men.

MALCOLM

They were men who you used the "N" word quite frequently to describe.

VISITOR

Everyone did in those days, but I never used it in speeches or debates, but that's no excuse. The important point is that I did come to despise slavery. Many Whites could not let it go because it continued to be part of the economic foundation for much of the country. I knew it was a dependency that was crippling and separating our country. Most importantly, in the eyes of God, it was wrong.

RFK

Is it true that your family didn't own any slaves?

VISITOR

We were lucky because we were too poor, so we were afforded the luxury of not committing such an immoral act, of purchasing slaves.

MALCOLM

History is made more palatable over the years. People shape facts to conform to their own wants and needs. For example, you have come to be known as the "Great Emancipator" to some people. But to those die-hard confederates, it is said that they think you were the "biggest war criminal." You made it clear, however, that your main mission was to preserve the Union. So, again, why come here this evening? I feel like you are insulting this occasion to some degree.

VISITOR

You are right, I did once proclaim: *If I could save the Union, without freeing the slaves, I would do it. If I could do it by freeing some and leaving others alone, I would do that. What I do about slavery and the coloured race, I do because I believe it would help to save the Union.* It just had to be done this way. This comment was looked upon unfavorably by many Africans, yet I had the unlikeliest of supporters among them after saying this. But I believe that this man knew that my heart was partly in the right place.

RFK

Who would that be?

MALCOLM

Frederick Douglass.

VISITOR

Yes, this was another turning point for me, my relationship with the abolitionist Frederick Douglass.

MALCOLM

(In a sarcastic tone.) It's a wonder he didn't show up here tonight.

DR. KING

How well did you know him? I've heard some stories about your relationship with him. How true are those tales?

VISITOR

We got to know one another pretty well. He helped me to see slaves as full human beings. Although the main thrust of my message was to save the Union, Douglass understood that if the policy was also to free the slaves, it would not have worked at all. Douglass saw the war as one being fought for slavery or freedom. As a result of the Proclamation, Governor John Andrew of Massachusetts raised the 54th regiment of Colored Troops and Douglass helped to recruit two companies of men, including his two sons. I was much taken and impressed with Douglass.

DR. KING
Tell me more about the relationship? How were you taken with him?

VISITOR
Douglass came to visit me at the White House. He had a lot of influential friends in Washington, and they put him in contact with me. Douglass wanted me to make changes in the way the Colored Troops were being treated. Among his concerns was the lack of promotions and the pay differences between White and Colored soldiers. Also he was deeply concerned about the way many Black Union soldiers were being captured and re-enslaved in the South.

JFK
Interesting, those requests he made must have seemed strange at a time like that when freedom was the impending issue. How did you react to his demands?

VISITOR
The fact that he would seek equality for Black people gave me a lot to think about. He made me search my soul, and I realized that under the surface, the skin, that all human life had the desire and need for freedom. Everything began to dawn on me very clearly. I learned that Douglass and I had a lot in common, including our very humble beginnings.

DR. KING
I had always found it difficult to understand that most people could not grasp that elementary concept. Men are all bone and flesh beneath the surface.

VISITOR
I appreciated the lesson that Douglass taught me. I could not respect him more, even if he were White. From him I learned that the myth of black inferiority was, indeed, a myth. But how do you change the hearts and minds of a nation that has long relished power and control over another group of people, especially when the basis for control is economic. The superiority of the White

race and the growth of the economy in the south depended on and needed Blacks to be the inferior race. Black skin had long since become a sign of servitude.

JFK

I was saying something similar to that effect before you came in. How a moral act can be so unpopular among so many? Something that is so clear before your own eyes but distorted by so many. But, I think you already answered that question, Dr. King. It is greed and power over others that corrupt the soul.

MALCOLM

I also said earlier that the truth is not easy to recognize. The mind can play so many tricks. You have to figure out the mystery of life. What I saw and experienced in my life led me to believe that all White people were blue-eyed devils. However, after my trip to Mecca, my experiences led me to truth. Anyone can be a devil, blue-eyed or brown-eyed or any other color. It's important to question things that do not make sense.

> (They all turn to look at the radio as two more states come in, one for Obama and one for McCain, Oregon and Idaho, respectively.)

VISITOR

Obama won a seat in the Illinois senate, and I couldn't. Gentlemen, I have a feeling that this will be a big night.

JFK

Yes, but we will have to wait a bit longer. It doesn't seem that it will be a close race, but let's wait until they call it to make it official.

RFK

Sir, (Referring to the VISITOR.) we were here simply amusing ourselves with stories of our untimely demise before you showed up. It seems as if we have much in common.

DR. KING

We all left our earthly lives during the tumultuous sixties, we all had the opportunity to participate in the Civil Rights struggle. And what was that other thing, Malcolm, that you were about to say before our Visitor showed up.

MALCOLM

Well, other than a conspiracy-theory behind each of our assassinations, we were all on the verge of something wonderful connected to our passions while in service to mankind. I think that's what I was about to say before our visitor showed up and gave us his elaborate yet plausible explanation of race relations during the nineteenth century.

VISITOR

I am so glad that you find my account satisfactory since I did pay the ultimate price for the stance I took. My demise is attributed to the "peculiar institution" of slavery. And what a conspiracy that turned out to be.

JFK

So, our dear Visitor, we understand your connection to Civil Rights as being the Great Emancipator, but, why, truly, did you want to be here tonight? We are of a different era and never made your acquaintance during our lives. Although I must admit that this is a great honor for me to personally make your acquaintance, and I would look forward to sharing the rest of the evening with a former president, like myself.

VISITOR

I believe the further reason for being here may become evident in time.

DR. KING

Would you tell us about your untimely demise then? That's what we were discussing.

VISITOR

I did hear some of that conversation when I arrived. I stood outside the door listening before I knocked to make certain I was in the right place. I heard the Senator (Referring to RFK.) discussing the last days of his earthly life.

RFK

Yes, I was saying how I hadn't expected it to happen because I was on the verge of something very promising. Were you also on the verge of a breakthrough at the time of your demise?

VISITOR

No, I think I already had my breakthrough. The Civil War had been fought and won by the North and the Union was intact. States' rights were relegated to those of the nation. Slavery was at long last over. But, I still had many challenges before me. The country had been torn apart and had to be rebuilt. I was very much looking forward to the task. There was one thing that I did not count on. You see, I thought the Civil War was truly over, and it wasn't.

JFK

What do you mean it wasn't over? It was done. You were able to get the 13th Amendment through the Senate and, finally, the house.

VISITOR

No, don't you see. The war wasn't done until that fateful day when I was shot.

JFK

I don't understand.

VISITOR

I was the last casualty of the Civil War, as some have said. I had many plans to rebuild a stronger and more unified Union. In that, yes, I was on the verge of participating in something truly wonderful. And like all of you, I was assassinated. But the process of freedom had unfolded and could not be undone. The slaves were free, but I did not think that the road to freedom for Africans would be so long and the pace so slow. Tonight after more than 140 years, I am hopeful that the task will be accomplished.

JFK
Did you know that it was going to happen that day at the theatre?

VISITOR
I did not want to be the first presidential assassination and set a trend. I always knew that I had embarked on a new direction for the country and that is always, in many respects, a dangerous mission, especially in this case. The war was over, but the country was divided. The ill feelings would not go away overnight.

JFK
You paved the way for me, didn't you? You were the first president to be assassinated?

VISITOR
It's humorous in a way. I actually had a dream that I would be assassinated, even though it had not ever happened to a president. I told my body guard about the dream. The die-hard Confederates and Copperheads detested me, so I felt that I was reading this into my subconscious. I did not think, if it ever did happen, that it would be in a theatre of all places. That evening I felt I could relax, let my guard down, and enjoy an evening with my wife, who was sitting there beside me.

DR. KING
I didn't suspect it either; otherwise, I would not have stepped out on that balcony.

VISITOR
It was April 14, 1865, and I was with my wife at the Ford's Theatre in Washington, D.C., as you all well know. *Our American*

Cousin was playing. It was a farcical play. It was well into the 2nd scene of Act III, and the character Asa Trenchard was about to utter one of the funniest lines of the play when I became slightly aware that someone had jumped into the State Box, number 7 that Mary and I sat in. The theatre rang out with just some of the loudest laughter. And I laughed too, only for a second because that's when I felt the shot to my head at point-blank range. It turned out to be a single shot, round slug 0.44 from a caliber Derringer. I was in a coma for several hours.

> (JFK, RFK, DR. KING, AND MALCOLM gather
> around the VISITOR to comfort him.)

JFK

Are you okay? It can be traumatic reliving such a violent event.

VISITOR

No, I am just still a bit confused by it all. (Looking dazed.) I was just sitting there enjoying the show, and then it was all over. I understand that it was a premeditated conspiracy involving many others, and it took me by surprise.

RFK

Clearly, it was an unexpected event because just a week or so earlier, Lee had surrendered to Grant, and the country was finally looking forward to peaceful times ahead. Then out of nowhere your assassination and the attempted one against your secretary of state's life.

DR. KING

I believe that the Reconstruction period may have been a lot different had you been around to lead the effort.

JFK

Perhaps, it would have been different, but the country was still so fragile. No one wanted the South to try its hand at secession again.

RFK

There is no doubt that the country was shaken after the assassination because it was the first time in the history of the young nation that this had happened. All through the land, it has been written, there was grief, rage, and despair. Your legacy endured, and you even turned out to be one of the more popular presidents of the country.

MALCOLM

My esteemed Visitor, I would be honored to share the rest of the evening with you. This is off the subject . . . . (Referring to the VISITOR.) But as I studied your life when I was reading all of those books in the prison library, I often wondered if you were Jewish? Not that it matters or anything. I was just curious. Some people have said that you might have even had some Black ancestors. What do you say to all of this?

VISITOR

Malcolm, I am so sorry to disappoint you, but the truth of the matter is that I do not know. If there is any truth to those rumors, my parents kept it a secret for obvious reasons. But I'd be proud if I did.

MALCOLM

Well, just so you know, Abraham sounds a bit Jewish to me.

> (The discussion is interrupted as the radio announcer is ready to make the call. The men gather around the radio. The announcer is calling the winner of the election Barack Obama.)

DR. KING

Do you know what this means?

JFK

No, please tell us. What does it mean to you Dr. King?

DR. KING
The train has just pulled into the station of the Promised Land. America's promise or the check that was returned marked insufficient funds has just been honored. We had two very qualified candidates and the selection of a Black man has been made because he is deemed more fitting for the job, not just by minorities but also Whites. Life will not be any different for the average Black man when he wakes up tomorrow, but there is promise.

JFK
I agree with you Dr. King. This is the beginning of the country's progress toward a post-racist society. The country will have to continue to work on eradicating all forms of racism, discrimination, and other forms of bigotry.

RFK
This is a major advancement for the principles of freedom and social justice. As I once said: *We all struggle to transcend the cruelties and the follies of mankind. That struggle will not be won by standing aloof and pointing a finger; it will be won by action, by those who commit their every resource of mind and body to the education and improvement and help of their fellow man.* Courage brings change. My courageous brothers, I have been glad to share this magical evening with you.

MALCOLM
I wish only the best for America. I hope now the issue of race will begin to fade into the past. From the fields where the slaves toiled to the revolts and rebellions, my ancestors have been partially redeemed tonight.

VISITOR
(Looks around at everyone.) It should be very apparent why we are all here together this evening. Our best efforts have been realized and our sacrifices made whole. There were times when we wavered or succumbed to the wrong truths, but fate and our belief in mankind, though difficult at times, allowed us to

persevere. Let's hope America can learn the lessons of this long and difficult experience. We have a Minister and a Reverend in our midst. Let us join in prayer for our country and the world to seek out further peace and reconciliation. Let there continue to be brave and honest men who, even at great cost, stand against the currents of injustice.

> (The five men join shoulder to shoulder in a circle. DR. KING has retrieved his minister's shawl, and he and MALCOLM X lead the group in prayer. Clouds obstruct the view of the men as President-Elect Obama's victory speech is broadcast in and out of frequency on the radio.)

PRESIDENT-ELECT OBAMA'S VOICE

If there is anyone out there who still doubts that America is a place where all things are possible; who still wonders if the dream of our founders is alive in our time; who still questions the power of our democracy, tonight is your answer . . . It's been a long time coming, but tonight, because of what we did on this day, in this election, at this defining moment, change has come to America . . . As Lincoln said to a nation far more divided than ours, "We are not enemies, but friends . . . Though passion may have strained, it must not break our bonds of affection." And, to those Americans whose support I have yet to earn, I may not have won your vote, but I hear your voices, I need your help, and I will be your president, too . . . Thank you, God bless you, and may God bless the United States of America.

THE END